# STRING THEM UP

## WILLIAM STERLING

**Let the world know:**
**#IGotMyCLPBook!**

**Crystal Lake Publishing**
**www.CrystalLakePub.com**

Join the Crystal Lake community today
on our newsletter and Patreon!
https://linktr.ee/CrystalLakePublishing

Download our latest catalog here.
https://geni.us/CLPCatalog



ISBN: 978-1-957133-59-1

Cover art:
Ben Baldwin—www.benbaldwin.co.uk

Layout:
Lori Michelle—www.theauthorsalley.com

Proofread by:
Paula Limbaugh

# WELCOME

## TO ANOTHER

## CRYSTAL LAKE PUBLISHING

## CREATION

# PREFACE

**WE FEAR THE** dark not for what it is, but because of what it hides from us. We fear it because there is potential in those shadows which we dread to ever face directly. Left alone, stranded by the absence of light, our imagination takes over and we assume that we hear, we see, we *feel* all manner of ghosts, goblins, and nameless evils shrouded therein. Each one searching for us, finding us, closing in on us while we wait there, alone, defenseless.

But what if it isn't the dark we should fear? What if, instead, we should cower from the light? What if, when the light finally shows us all those things which the shadows have kept hidden, their reality turns out to be *too much*?

Though our imaginations can summon unspeakable horrors all on their own, what of those things beyond our minds' comprehension?

How quickly would we succumb to madness when confronted with everything the darkness has kept shrouded from us?

What if all this time, the darkness has been our shield, our protector, our blessing?

What if we aren't ready to see what truly lurks beyond that veil?

# NEW BEGINNINGS

**AN UNSEASONABLY COOL** wind blew through Hollow Hills, scattering leaves and prompting shadows to dance across the steps of Sinclair Redford's new home.

Sinclair stood by his car, arms crossed over his chest, a deep sadness in his eyes as he surveyed the house in front of him. He kept trying, and failing, to see past the things that this new "home" lacked.

Claire.

Max.

He had hoped that moving all the way out here might somehow fill the void they'd left behind. Or, at least, he had hoped that the move might dull the sting of their absence. But as he hugged himself, trying to ward off the chill, Sinclair understood just how misplaced and naive that hope had been.

The memories of his lost family couldn't simply be misplaced, lost among the strange rooms or the unfamiliar halls of a new location. There was no true solace to be found in a different living room, different furniture. Even standing in the driveway, staring in the face of his fresh start, the memory of Claire and Max's bodies, splayed out, broken and mangled on the morgue table, burned just as fresh in Sinclair's mind as always. He would be haunted by those images, that pain, forever. East Coast, West Coast, inner-city, or podunk rural outskirts, their deaths would follow him to the ends of the Earth.

Ignorance of loss, of suffering, was a bliss that he had taken for granted for so many years. It was a bliss which he had moved a hundred miles to try to reclaim. But it turned out that unhealing, festering blip on his timeline wouldn't, couldn't be escaped so easily as Sinclair had hoped.

He imagined he could still hear the blare of the fire trucks echoing along with the racket of the grasshoppers that sang in his new, overgrown lawn.

Fuck.

Sinclair had spent so many years setting up the dominoes of his life just the right way.

He'd landed a stable job. Sure, being a detective had put him face to face with the monstrous pits of human existence from time to time, but it had paid the bills each month.

He'd married a beautiful, loving woman who meant the world to him.

He'd had a rambunctious, but sweet, child.

He'd had a plan to retire in just a hair over a decade with the pair of them, and he'd already picked out the general area where he would build a lakeside cabin. Where he would spend the rest of his days in bliss.

The hell had that all been for now, though?

All of his plans, all of his expectations, had been a feeble, naive house of cards, built by an idiot who thought he could keep the table from wobbling underneath.

He saw that now.

Sinclair took a deep breath, rubbed his hands on the outside of his pockets in a frustrated gesture, and tried to block these thoughts out.

He needed to focus on the move. The clean start. The new job. He crinkled his nose and scanned up and down the street, taking in the rest of his surroundings as the back of the moving truck slammed closed. One of the movers, his name tag read 'B.T.', came waddling around the truck's side with a stack of alternating pink, yellow, and white forms.

"Standard stuff," the mover said as he passed the papers to Sinclair. "Just says that we didn't break anything as we moved it in."

"Well . . . did you?"

"Did we what?" The mover cocked an eyebrow.

"Break anything."

"'Course not," B.T. said with a Cheshire grin.

Sinclair glanced towards the house, considering verifying B.T.'s words, but the tedium of checking every square inch of every item that they might have nicked or scraped would have been too much for Sinclair. He wanted to be left alone so that he could pass out for the rest of the afternoon. For the rest of eternity if the devil was willing to take him.

With barely a cursory glance at the words on the page, Sinclair signed the mover's forms and passed them back.

B.T. tipped his cap and within seconds the truck was screeching away like it was trying to escape.

Well, shit.

With that sort of an exit, they had definitely broken something.

Or maybe the mover just wanted to get away from Sinclair and his tragic energy as fast as possible.

Depression wasn't contagious, but it sure drove people away as if it was.

Just hopefully it wasn't any of Max's things. If they'd broken Max's rocking horse, then Sinclair would hunt the movers down and gut them.

Sinclair hefted a duffle bag from the back seat of his car. It was heavy, stuffed to the gills with the essentials that Sinclair had lugged on his road trip. A change of clothes for his homeless night in a hotel, deodorant, and mini bottles of shampoo all rattled around in the main sack as his toothbrush jabbed his side through a mesh pocket. Sinclair wandered up the cracked sidewalk, through the knees-high grass and weeds in the front yard, and past his Corolla with the tire that had blown on the very last mile into town.

Sinclair frowned back at the tire as he trudged up the short steps to his new home. Did he have a spare in the trunk? Sinclair shrugged, mentally. Even if he had a spare, the car could wait. There were too many memories in those seat cushions that Sinclair needed space from. The car could sit in the driveway for a while, and maybe the ghosts it held would get bored, go wandering off before Sinclair needed to slide behind the wheel again.

The last day in the car had been torture. Seeing Max in the rearview mirror at every red light. Smelling Claire's perfume whenever the windows were closed.

Sinclair turned his eyes away from the sedan, back to the front door.

His new house looked the same way that Sinclair felt. Abandoned. Unkempt. Falling apart at the seams. The siding hosted a forest of mold, one gutter hung awkwardly from the second-floor window, just above the master bedroom, and Sinclair would be damned if there wasn't a leak in the attic, judging from the state of the shingles on the roof.

A hovel of a home for a shell of a man to wither away in. They were the perfect pair.

At least the air conditioning worked, Sinclair noted as he swung the door open. That would be a blessing come April against the oppressive Georgian heat. He made his way slowly through the rooms of the house, growing more and more certain with each room that the movers had probably broken *multiple* somethings, with each box and piece of furniture casually tossed into corners, rolled onto their sides, or stacked five-boxes high.

Damn it.

He kept moving, slowly learning the layout of the house he'd never stepped foot in before. Johnny had picked a realtor to help handle all of that for Sinclair. Finding a house, haggling the price down on account of its fixer-upper status. Johnny knew these people. Knew who to trust and who to call bullshit on when they came to the negotiating table.

Or, at least, Sinclair had thought that his friend was good for that.

On the main floor was a dining room, a living room, and a kitchen. The pictures online had exaggerated how large each room was, but Sinclair didn't care all that much. It was just him in the house. How much room would he really need?

Upstairs were two claustrophobic guest bedrooms, balanced out by a master bedroom which was reasonably large. Sinclair noted a large brown stain on the back wall which hadn't been disclosed in the home inspection, but he shrugged it off. Who cared?

Sinclair wandered silently back across the upstairs landing and entered one of the guest bedrooms, clocking the rocking horse which looked blessedly unharmed, as he wandered up to a box labeled "MAX'S THINGS." He squatted down next to the box, blinking back a tear and fingering the edge of the packing tape.

He wanted to check on his boy's things.

Really, the movers could have broken any of Sinclair's personal belongings and he wouldn't have given two shits. But Max's stuff was irreplaceable.

He squatted there, on his haunches, for a long minute. Blinking. Scared. Until finally he pulled his finger away from the tape.

He couldn't look in the box yet. This was supposed to be a new beginning. A fresh start. Sinclair couldn't let his first action in this new home be tainted by the discovery that one of Max's favorite toys had been broken, or that his baseball cards had been bent. Sinclair left the room and closed the door behind him.

Maybe tomorrow.

Maybe.

But not today.

Sinclair considered the huge unpacking job that awaited him. What did he need to tackle first? Pots and pans so that he could feed himself? Unpacking the bedroom so that he would have somewhere to sleep?

Both sounded exhausting.

Maybe he would just pull the plastic off the couch and pass out down there.

Instead, Sinclair's hand wandered into his pocket and he pulled out his phone to glance at the alerts.

Three missed calls from Johnny Thompson in the past hour.

Sinclair sighed, wandered back downstairs, and slopped himself unceremoniously onto the pile of plastic wrapping which hid his couch.

It had been Johnny's idea for Sinclair to move out here. To get away from the hustle and the bustle of Charlotte where every street corner and restaurant harbored memories of his dead family.

"You need a place to start fresh," Johnny had said.

It was the same thing his Sergeant had said as he signed Sinclair's transfer papers.

It was the same thing his mother had said when he talked to her on the phone.

The same thing that the court appointed therapist had told him during their final session.

Honestly, if one more person had told him to leave, then Sinclair might have stayed in Charlotte out of sheer spite. But here he was, bunking up in the outskirts of Hollow Hills, Georgia, in a house of ill repair, trying to sweep the shattered dreams of his former life under a rug.

. . . Rug . . .

Where was his rug?

Damn movers.

Sinclair thumbed the green button beside Johnny's name. Maybe Johnny could bring him food. Take one thing off his to-do list.

Johnny was in Sinclair's new driveway within ten minutes.

# HEY, JOHNNY

**"HEY HEY HEY!"** Johnny shouted. He knocked on the door but entered without waiting for Sinclair to greet him.

Sinclair groaned, half-jokingly, as he rose to greet his old partner.

"Johnny. Good to see you," Sinclair hugged Johnny and slapped him once on the back. Johnny had let himself go a bit in the three years since he left Charlotte, Sinclair noted. What had once been a hefty dad bod had bloomed a no-kidding pot belly, and Johnny had grown something that resembled a beard across 85% of his chin. His uniform was wrinkled to hell, but at least his badge shone from a semi-recent polishing.

Johnny squeezed Sinclair until his back popped.

"My friend! How was the drive!?"

"Not too bad. These old back roads are hell, though. I'll need to get some new tires for sure."

"This the new place Shannon got for you?"

"Yup."

"It's . . . " Johnny's voice trailed off as he struggled for something positive to say.

"As ugly as your mother?" Sinclair offered, and Johnny broke out in a burst of his characteristically good-natured, full-body laughter. He pretended to punch at Sinclair and threw a jab into the open air.

"Yeah. You and Shan didn't go for the glitz OR the glamor, did you?"

"Didn't think I'd need to. Thought maybe a fixer-upper could keep my mind occupied whenever I wasn't at work."

"Well, you certainly found the most fixer of all the uppers, huh? Seriously though, there's some good guys around town who can lend you a hand with stuff once you get to know them. Biggest lumber mill on the east coast. I'm sure the Gattis Family will set you up with some new flooring for dirt cheap. You'll learn quick, but around here almost anything can get done for a couple I.O.U.s and cold beers."

"Hell of a lot different than Charlotte, huh?"

"Ah-yup. You have no idea."

Sinclair saw a strange look pass across his friend's face, but he was too tired to ask questions. Instead, he turned around to give Johnny the grand tour of his new place. It took all of three minutes, and Johnny had a wise-crack or a joke to accompany each new room as it was revealed.

"Kitchen looks like it hosted both World Wars. Guess it's a good thing you don't know how to cook anyhow, huh?"

"Living room is nice. Your little 12-inch plasma would probably take up most of that wall!"

"Closet under the stairs. Nice. We'll let you crawl in there, carve a lightning bolt on your forehead and let you pretend you're special."

Sinclair rolled his eyes at each jab, retorting with his own snipes whenever he could think of them.

Upstairs, he didn't open the door to Max's room.

Johnny didn't ask about it.

Johnny didn't joke about the picture of Sinclair and Claire lying safely beside the bed either.

Even Johnny knew when things were off limits.

That awareness was a big reason Sinclair had liked Johnny back in the big city. That, and the fact that Johnny had a modicum of honor within him. Even in the den of snakes that was Charlotte PD, Johnny had always tried to do the right thing.

"Well hell, old bud. What do you want to do?" Johnny asked as they ended the tour, standing in the master bedroom. He was staring curiously at the stained back wall, and Sinclair could sense the beginnings of a joke forming in his mind, but instead Johnny launched into "Want a hand getting all this stuff set up? Or do you want to head into town? Get a sense of your new stomping grounds and a bite to eat?"

Sinclair surveyed the jungle of boxes. He thought about all the memories which would be unearthed with each unfolding of cardboard flaps.

He wasn't ready for that yet.

It was time for new beginnings. Just like the world had mandated.

"Yeah. Let's check out the town, huh?"

"I'll drive. Looks like that pothole on Towns Street got a hold of your old beater on the way in, huh?"

"Yeah. Among other things."

"Want me to give you a hand changing it?"

"No." Sinclair said, glancing out the window at the remnant of his past life, sitting slumped and broken in the driveway. Visions of Claire smiling at him from the passenger seat while Max sang in the back overwhelmed him in a rush, leaving Sinclair feeling uncomfortable, dizzy. He blinked and ground his teeth, maintaining his composure around his old friend, his new boss, as he turned quickly away from the window.

"Yeah. You're right."

Johnny was nodding, pretending not to notice Sinclair struggling. Calling attention to the way Sinclair's lip trembled would have embarrassed him. Man-code prevailed. Just ignore the emotions until they go away.

Eyes averted; Johnny twirled his keys around his ring finger.

"Food first. But remember, I only offer to help with shit like changing tires once in a blue moon. I gave you a chance to get help and you passed. Must still be as stupid as you ever were."

Johnny nudged Sinclair in the ribs as the pair made their way back downstairs, and the jab tricked a smile across Sinclair's face. It felt good to be reunited with his old coworker, even under the circumstances. Good enough to dull the sting of the memories of Max, if just for a moment.

They piled into the beige truck with SHERIFF printed on the side in big, brown letters, and rolled out of the driveway. Sinclair made a point of not looking at his car, or the house, as they drove off.

# THE HOLLOW HILLS HAVE EYES. EARS. MOUTHS.

HOLLOW HILLS WAS picturesque, stereotypical, small-town USA. It had a main street that would look great on a postcard and people who sipped lemonade with each other on hot summer days. It was the type of place where kids still rode their bikes to school. Where you could probably still get a milkshake for a nickel at the corner store if you asked real nice. Or at least, that's the impression it gave to the few visitors who passed through each year. The reality was, like it was in most small towns, much more complicated.

The town had started as a trading post for mountain men from Blue Ridge to peddle the pelts, game, and whatever else they had shot, killed, hooked, lined, or sinkered back in ye olden days. It grew a fair bit when the Gattis family moved in and opened a small, moderately successful sawmill which attracted men who were desperate for work in the mid-1800s. Then the town just, in a way, gave up on itself. The ambitions of the people who lived there never expanded beyond a desire for one main road and a couple of niche shops. Those few kids and teenagers who were cursed with passion or dreams eventually left Hollow Hills for college and they never came back. Which was A-OK with the lemonade sippers in their rocking chairs.

People with ambition tended to complicate things.

Working too hard tended to complicate things.

It was best to just kick back and enjoy the simple life. That's what the lemonade sippers reckoned. So even as the world around them evolved, Hollow Hills kept itself willfully excluded from the mechanisms of the modern era.

Johnny tried to explain all of this to Sinclair as they drove around.

There was the Post Office- still trying its best to stave off the influence of Amazon and their two-day shipping.

There was the small local theater. It had been built in the mid-1900s by a kid who thought he could bring "culture" to the town, and who had later been run off for his (to quote Mr. Trelawney) "unacceptable efforts to corrupt the youths."

There was the defunct Toy Shop, its doors closed for the last few years, the toymaker retired and living on the town's edge.

It was all so quaint.

It was all so manicured and picturesque.

Sinclair struggled to decide how he felt about it. The culture shock coming from Charlotte was going to give him whiplash. But wasn't that the point? To immerse himself in something wholly different from where he had been? To reset his frame of mind so that he could reinvent himself? Restart his life?

Sinclair adjusted the A/C to stop himself from sweating through his nice shirt as Johnny pulled into a parking spot; the very last spot along Hollow Hill's long row of brick-faced buildings.

"And here you have it. The gem of Hollow Hills. Citadel of righteousness and legal execution standing tall in the unruly wilds of Northeast Georgia. The Hollow Hills Sheriff's Station!" Johnny announced the sight with an obviously mocking enthusiasm.

Their station looked exactly like the rest of the buildings on main street: Its roof hung low over its second story. The bricks had faded to dull reds and browns, their edges and corners worn away by decades of rainfall. 'Re-Elect Mayor Bellman' signs were posted in the narrow strip of grass which separated the parking spaces from the sidewalks and the only thing that differentiated this building from the others seemed to be the bars on the windows.

Sinclair stepped out of Johnny's truck and began to approach the station's front door, but his friend stepped in front of him.

"Woah woah woah. Hey hey hey. No. You just got here. You're not even moved in yet. Work can wait until tomorrow. Clyde's on duty right now, and if we distract him for even one second, then any productivity he might have stumbled across will be derailed for the rest of the afternoon. Get back. Back I say!" Johnny seemed to be half joking, half serious, judging by the smirk on his face and the way he pushed Sinclair away.

"That's not why we're out here. The bar, my man! The bar! You need food. Not work."

Sinclair turned on his heel and read the sign across the road. 'PADDY'S PUB' looked just like the Sheriff's station.

"Their food any decent?" Sinclair asked as Johnny pushed him away from the station.

"Hell no. But it does technically count as food. How many calories are in a bucket of grease? Never mind. Doesn't matter. In, in, in, before O'Hare sees the car out front and comes to talk my ear off about some non-issue."

"You sound like you suck as a Sheriff."

Johnny chuckled, but it sounded forced. For a moment, Sinclair saw the shadow of sadness race across his friends' face, just like it had at Sinclair's house. But again, Johnny regained his composure quickly.

Sinclair had struck a nerve. Bad way to get reintroduced to his old friend. Sinclair didn't pry, same as Johnny hadn't pried in the master bedroom.

"Yeah yeah. Judge me all you want tomorrow after you've met the town. For now though, *in*."

The double doors of Paddy's Pub were heavy and slow to open. The place was packed. An old-school jukebox pumped classic rock from the back corner of the joint, and just about every booth and barstool was occupied by stereotypical looking small town yuppies, all of whom looked over to see who had joined their ranks. They nodded pleasantly towards their Sheriff, then paused to take stock of the newcomer. Conversations stopped. Even the jukebox seemed to skip a beat.

Sinclair tried to smile back at them all, but he knew the look appeared forced. What did he have to smile about?

A hostess emerged from the shadows to the side and one by one the townsfolk turned back to their previous conversations. A new song started on the jukebox as Sinclair and Johnny slid across the sticky plastic seats of the last remaining booth.

"Burger and a Bud like usual?" the hostess asked Johnny with a heavy southern drawl as she walked them to their seats. Apparently, the lines between hostess and waitress were blurry here.

"You know me so well, darlin'." Johnny responded, adopting an exaggerated drawl of his own. Sinclair cocked an eyebrow at that, but Johnny just laughed and shook his head.

"And how about you?"

"Water and a burger."

"You trying to go dry?" Johnny asked.

"No. Just wary of the locals seeing their brand-new deputy getting drunk in public."

"Shit, Sinclair. You really don't 'get' this town yet. They see you not drinking they'll trust you even less than if you were on call and plastered. Staying sober means you're trying to focus. Means you're working hard on something. And if the Sheriff is working hard on something, that means trouble's afoot. Does it make sense? No. Is that the way things roll around here? Yes," Johnny said. "You're off duty. You're good. Promise. Get my guy a Bud also! I'm paying, if that's really what this is about."

"It's not."

"Well, whatever. Get Sheriff's Deputy Redford here a water and a Bud. Drink the water if you want, but at least have the Bud on the table. It'll help with the optics and all that."

Johnny winked, half at Sinclair, half at the woman standing over them with her lips pursed. The hostess/waitress scratched something out on her notepad, nodded, and sauntered off towards the kitchen in the back.

Sinclair rolled his eyes. He had forgotten how pushy Johnny was. It came from a place of good intentions, but damn if it wasn't exhausting sometimes.

A couple who had been sitting in a nearby booth rose as the waitress walked away. They came over and greeted the Sheriff, then introduced themselves to Sinclair as Mr. and Mrs. Gattis. They ran the sawmill, apparently, and they had three dogs which Mrs. Gattis whipped out pictures of, as if Sinclair had asked to see them.

Sinclair returned their salutations and tried to come across as amicable and neighborly as possible until they left him alone and went back to their booth. They sat and another group of four rose from a table nearby to fill the conversational void. Mr. and Mrs. Tillman, with their kids Rosemary and Shelby. They sat. Another family stood. And on and on, like a carousel of introductions until finally, blessedly, Sinclair and Johnny's food arrived, breaking the pattern of interaction.

Sinclair sighed and downed the last of the beer which he did, by that point, feel like he needed. "Jesus. Everybody around here's so nice it's almost suffocating. You get the same treatment when you rode in?"

"Aw, yeah," Johnny laughed around a mouthful of hamburger. "That won't stop for a couple of months. People are gonna be showing up on your doorstep for weeks with apple pies and peach pies and cherry pies trying to make nice with the new guy."

"Sounds exhausting."

"It is."

"Nice though."

Johnny crinkled his eyebrows and chewed for a minute before responding.

"You know how back in Charlotte everybody was just a stuck-up asshole openly?"

"Uh huh."

"Not the case around here. Here in the real South, people like to fake nice. They'll smile at you and offer you a drink and if you don't look too close at their smiles you can almost believe that they're genuine. For the heavy majority of people around here, that porcelain mask is all they'll ever look for. Those people will just kick back on their front porches with a lemonade, glance at the mostly disarming smiles of their neighbors, and they'll be happy as all get out. "

"But not us, huh?"

Johnny shook his head and polished off his beer. He shifted his weight around and smiled, giving his badge a playful flick.

"These people are petty as hell, and the gossip mill is a fucking nightmare, but 99 times out of 100 things seem to end with little more than neighbors not talking to one another or a divorce lawyer getting paid. Rarely ever boils over into action for us, which is for the best I guess."

He stopped, got a faraway look in his eye as he remembered something, then laughed.

"Heh. Actually. You know what? No. Last year Mr. Good threw a bucket of paint thinner onto Ms. Ratley's garden. It was such a big deal that we're still talking about it . . . what . . . 13 months later? So make it 98 times out of a hundred things end in vows of silence. Every now and then we get a garden variety planticides."

Johnny's chuckles died off as he took a swig of his drink. He set the glass back on the table and ran his finger through the condensation, the sad look back in his eyes.

"You'd think in a town like this a Sheriff might get a real chance to do some good. Make a difference. But there's just not that many chances to do good."

"Not like in Charlotte where there were chances aplenty."

Johnny shook his head.

"Here we're just a big fish in a clean, boring pond versus Charlotte where we were a small as shit fish in an ocean full of shit. No way either fish will do much of anything with their lives except live 'em."

Sinclair lowered his eyes and tapped on his coaster. He understood his boss's apathy all too well.

One beer wasn't going to be enough for tonight after all. He caught the waitresses' eye, twirled a finger in the air, and before he could even drop his hand back down another glass had arrived. This one was twice as large as the first. A 64 ounce mug or something ridiculous like that. Sinclair didn't care. Any of his reservations about drinking in front of the public had leaked away.

"So . . . You wanna talk about Charlotte? Get it all off your chest? I heard the reports, and just . . . Damn. Sinclair. Nobody should ever have to go through that. I can't begin to imagine. If you don't want to talk about it, I get it. But you know. Open start. Clear the room. That sort of a thing?" Johnny stumbled through his offer to play therapist.

"I'd rather not. Not yet. I don't see the good in airing that out. Not like words could fix anything at this point. Sometimes things can't be fixed. Sometimes bad things happen and once they've happened then there's nothing you or the rest of the world can do but accept them. See them for what they are and learn how to live your life in the wreckage that got left behind."

Sinclair took a massive swig from his drink. Knocked out a fifth of it in a single pull.

"That's not what human nature wants us to do though, is it?" He continued. "Human nature wants us to fix, to repair, to revise. But there's no repairing the smell of my dead wife, her skin burst like a fucking Bratwurst; fat crackling in the furnace that our house became. There's no revising what happened to Max . . . There one second, gone the next . . . "

Sinclair's voice trailed off and he stared at his drink for a long, hard minute. Johnny sat, quietly for once, struggling to find the right words to say.

But there were no right words. There was nothing to be done. That was the worst part of Sinclair's point. Maybe that was his entire point. Shit. He'd done it again. Straight down the rabbit hole of self-hatred and loathing.

Sinclair tipped the second beer back and let it disappear down his throat, pounding the alcohol on purpose. Bidding the drink to drown out his thoughts.

"I think I should head home. See you tomorrow."

"I'll give you a ride," Johnny said, rising and eyeing the monstrous glass that Sinclair had just slammed. "You hit those beers that you didn't want pretty hard," Johnny said with a playful wink, trying to recover the mood and grateful to be saved from addressing Sinclair's philosophical waxing. "I'll show you the rest of town on the way. You have any clue where the grocery store is? Or the home supplies?"

"I'll find it. Town isn't that big."

"No. It sure isn't."

"Sinclair? I'm here for you, man. In any way you need me."

"I know it, bud. And, Johnny? Thanks. You've done wonders for me, just getting me out here. But for now I think I just need some sleep."

Johnny nodded.

A half hour later, Johnny pulled his truck into the driveway of Sinclair's new house.

Sinclair stepped carefully down from the passenger seat, watching as the world teetered beneath him. He'd slammed the beers too fast after staying sober for too long. His tolerance was down.

Maybe not the best way to start his tenure as the deputy.

It was dark by the time Sinclair managed to jiggle the keys to his house into their deadbolt, getting the contraption turned and open with an embarrassing amount of effort. Johnny had to help him up the stairs. Together, they dug through boxes until they found sheets and a pillow, and then Sinclair collapsed onto the mattress which the movers had tossed on the ground. Work was going to suck the next morning.

# GHOSTS

**SINCLAIR'S BLADDER WOKE** him just a little past three in the morning.

Johnny was gone, and all around him, the bare walls and the empty halls of the house seemed to watch him through the open doors. Sinclair stumbled, seemingly alone, into the master bathroom. He relieved himself, popped a few Tylenol to stave off the looming hangover, then stumbled back into the bedroom: navigating the unfamiliar territory with a graceless unease that exaggerated how drunk he really thought he was. His shin found the corner of a box of pictures and Sinclair flopped to the mattress, rolling around and pulling the sheets towards him.

There was a snag, the covers going taught when he pulled.

Sinclair wriggled a bit, trying not to steal too much of the sheets from his still-sleeping wife.

He gave up, resigning himself to sleeping bare and draped an arm affectionately across Claire's midriff. Sinclair squeezed his wife lightly, his eyes closed in the hopes that sleep might return to him quickly.

It didn't.

As Sinclair lay there for seconds, minutes, hours maybe even, he grew more and more conscious of how wrong this situation was. Slowly his half-asleep, half-drunk brain put the pieces together.

Claire was dead.

She had been dead since the fire. He had moved away from Charlotte because he kept seeing her ghost walking the halls of their house and now, here in Hollow Hills, she had emerged again.

Sinclair gave the form in bed with him another squeeze. Softer this time. More curiosity than affection. Flesh and bone shifted under his pressure, then settled back, limp, to their original positions. Sinclair recognized the smell of rot; spoiled meat forgotten in the back of a broken refrigerator.

He wanted to open his eyes. Wanted to see what lay in front of him, but at the same time, he dared not risk his sanity for the cost of a peek.

So he lay there.

The hours dragged into days. The days dragged into months. Still Sinclair lay, as still as the grave until his phone screamed its high-pitched jingle and startled him back to his senses.

Sinclair sat bolt-upright in bed, alone again save for the daylight streaming through the windows.

It was time for work.

Sinclair hustled down the stairs, grateful for the promise of something to do, a distraction from the poisoned well of his own mind.

# TRAINING DAY

**THE NEXT MORNING** Johnny picked Sinclair up promptly at 9:00. He had two steaming hot thermoses waiting in his truck's cup holders and a ham and egg biscuit in the passenger seat. Sinclair cast a disappointed, sad glance at his own hobbled car as he slid into Johnny's seat and grabbed the biscuit.

"Courtesy of Mama Jean's," Johnny said, nodding at the biscuit. "As far as hangover cures go, Mama's got the magic touch. Get some grease in you, newbie. We've got a town to meet." Sinclair buckled himself in, then gratefully forced down the grease bomb and caffeine chaser. He put some sunglasses on and tried to hide the effects of the previous night as well as possible, forcing himself to pay as much attention as he could to Johnny's descriptions of the town. The Sheriff took the corners slowly in the truck, pointing to most of the houses which they passed as he told stories of their residents.

"Some of these folk never leave their houses, so there's not much to know about them. They live out here in Hollow Hills instead of the big city for a reason. They don't want to be bothered, and they don't want nobody to bother them neither. I'd say probably 30% of the townsfolk around here you wont see or hear from unless there's a birth or a funeral to attend. And even then . . . well, some people just don't like company. But up here, the house with the red flowers under the windows? That's the Hammond house. You met them last night. They talk a lot, and I mean a *lot*, but they aren't ever going to actually do anything to get themselves in trouble."

Sinclair nodded, thinking that he needed to be taking notes about all this, but unwilling to drag out his notepad. Just the idea of scratching words down on a piece of paper while they drove was enough to make his stomach turn. He'd have to just keep listening and trying to soak it all in.

"Okay. Up here things get tricky. On the left, the house with the American Flag? that's the Archer's house. Or. Shit, no. Sorry. Not the Archer's house. It's the Kyle's house. Used to be the Archer's house until Mr. Archer got caught shacking up with Dorothy McClellan across the street. The house with the garden gnomes in the front yard, you see it? Yeah. That one. So Mrs. Archer kicked Mr. Archer out of the house and went back to her maiden name- Kyle. Missy Kyle."

"And the house with the garden gnomes is the Archer house now because Mr. Archer moved in with Dorothy?" Sinclair ventured a guess.

"Good try, but nope. Apparently Rick Archer tried to disavow his affair with Dorothy, saying she meant nothing to him in an attempt to win the old Mrs. Archer back, but it didn't work AND Mrs. Archer recorded the whole monologue and played it back for Dorothy McClellan to hear. So now good old Ricky boy has been scorned from both households."

"Where's the Archer household now, then?"

"Other side of town. Ricky got as far away from those two women and their venom as he could get while still staying local."

"So these are the Kyle house and the McClellan house now. And they both hate each other?"

"Actually? The ladies are best friends now. Mutual hatred of Ricky really gave them something to bond over."

"This town makes no sense."

"Nope. But you get used to it."

Sinclair groaned and wished he had stayed sober the night before, the way he had intended. This was all way too much to process while hungover. He felt the information sloshing about in his mind with nowhere to stick- the walls of his memory impermeable and coated with a slippery slathering of suds, hops, and barley.

Johnny took a hard left a little too fast and Sinclair pinched the bridge of his nose to stave off a bout of nausea. Tall, perfectly manicured hedges lined both sides of the road here with a long brick wall to help double up on the security.

"Here's the Mayor's place," Johnny explained, nodding to the series of 'Re-Elect Mayor Bellman' signs which infested the road's shoulder. A gap appeared between the ferns as Johnny drove past, revealing a heavy metal gate with a pristine white-painted plantation house set a quarter mile back from the road.

"Is he one of those 30 percenters who you were talking about? Doesn't want to be bothered?"

"Nah. He's actually out and about all the time. A bit obnoxious how under-foot he gets whenever something interesting starts happening. I suspect he'll be at the station later today to meet our newest shining star. New folks coming to town qualifies as an event worthy of the Mayor's graces."

"Super social guy who hides in his fortress of solitude each night, protected by a wrought iron fence? Doesn't sound like I'm gonna get along so well with him."

"Yeah. The estate's a bit much. Nobody else around here feels the need for a gated community vibe, but you know how rich people get. Name the last person you knew with any sort of money that just left it all hanging out there for others to walk up and take."

Sinclair scoffed, but couldn't argue.

"Besides. If Bellman gets your feathers ruffled, just wait till I show you the Rochester place."

"Who's Rochester?"

"Ah, shit."

Johnny pulled up to a stop sign and halted the truck, looking left and right up the road, deciding which way he wanted to turn.

"Let's jump the usual tour route. You deserve to see the town's looney bin before we waste time on anything else."

Again, Johnny swung the car around a little too fast, rerouting them away from town, and Sinclair had to battle down the effects of his hangover. Sinclair watched the hedges that marked the Mayor's estate fall away, getting replaced by tall, lush pines, thicker than he realized pines could get. Out here in the mountains, free from the pollution and influence of throngs of humans, nature flexed its power. Tree trunks that were six feet thick and still growing lined either side of the road, pressing in on either side of Johnny's truck as the asphalt road gave way to a two-lane dirt track which slimmed to a single-lane trail of rocks which slimmed to a point where Sinclair wasn't certain there really *was* a path they were following anymore. But Johnny held the truck steady, following some route which only he could see. A couple years spent out here in the boonies must have granted him special powers of vision which Sinclair hadn't adapted yet.

The truck's brakes squealed eventually and Johnny slowed the vehicle down to a stop at the base of two monstrous oaks, both long dead, whose branches formed an archway over a suddenly appearing strip of gravel which led up, up, and up the side of a mountain until it turned a corner. Signs had been nailed to the oaks:

**NO TRESPASSING**
**UNAUTHORIZED PERSONS WILL BE SHOT**

And the overly-welcoming:

**GET THE FUCK OFF MY PROPERTY**

Sinclair would have been tempted to smile at the brashness and the vulgarity of the signs if it wasn't for what hung in the branches overhead. Somehow, despite the branches being dead, and the impossible logistics of raising a ladder in a location like this, little dolls had been hung from both oaks like Christmas Ornaments.

Dead-eyed, mold-ridden, creepy as all hell Christmas Ornaments.

The lowest doll, and the one which Sinclair could see most clearly, resembled a little girl in a denim dress. The doll's eyes had fallen out years ago, and her hair had been ripped out in chunks, probably by some bird looking for materials for their nest. The string which held the doll was tied with a hangman's slipknot pulled down around the little doll's throat and the effect was ghastly enough to make Sinclair forget about his hangover. Forget Mama Jean's biscuits, the shock factor of the Rochester residence was Hollow Hills' true hangover cure.

"The hell . . . " was all Sinclair could think to blurt out.

"Right? So this guy . . . he's the one we've really gotta watch out for. The only one of the locals who might *actually* do some damage when he gets angry. 'Cause he's batty as shit. Just about everybody in town warned me about him when I first showed up, from Mayor Bellman, to Mrs. Arche- Miss Kyle, and everybody in between. Dude is a bad bag of attitude."

"You met him yourself?"

"Oh yeah. Couple of times. He doesn't come to town often, but when he does he hits two stops- grocery store and the old toy store he used to run. Always brings a doll with him, swaddled and in a carrier, like it's a real baby or something. The rest of the folk in town all try to give him a wide berth, but one way or another, somebody always rubs him the wrong way and I get called in to get the sum-bitch to stop shouting."

"Has he ever done anything besides shout?" Sinclair asked, his eyes still fixed on the dolls-gallows suspended above him.

"Nah. He's all bark. No bite. At least as far as I've seen. But still. There's something in his eyes. Even when he leaves to come back here, something ain't right. You get the feeling like one of these days he's finally gonna snap and we'll all be up in his trees alongside those little toys."

"That's dark as hell."

They sat in silence for a moment, listening to the dead tree creaking overhead as a slight breeze moved the branches back and forth, until Johnny let out a huge, hearty laugh that disrupted every bird and bug in the woods for a mile radius. He slapped Sinclair on the shoulder as Sinclair cringed away.

"I'm just screwin' with you, rookie. The dude's unhinged, sure. And I'm not wrong about the eyes. But for real, nothing ever happens here. E-ver," he enunciated as if Sinclair would have misunderstood him otherwise. "We show up, settle Rochester down, and he comes back up here every time without fail. Like a creepy Uncle who shows up for the holidays and we all just wait him out until he drives his racist ass home. Just make sure you talk real softly to him if you ever see a guy with a baby stroller full of freakin' Chucky dolls downtown, yeah?"

"Yeah. Sure. Alright."

Johnny spun the truck around.

"Time for the station?"

"Sure," Sinclair agreed. But for as long as he could see them, Sinclair didn't take his eyes off the dolls in the rearview mirror. Maybe it was just the wind, but he could have sworn he saw one of the little doll's arms lift, waving farewell to them as they drove off.

He could have sworn . . .

But no. That was stupid. Sinclair was just imagining things. It must have been the wind. Or the hangover. Or the sleep deprivation. Maybe just the stress of his first day on a new job. There were a mountain of logical reasons why Sinclair might have been seeing things. First his dead wife. Now a waving dolly.

He needed another cup of coffee, he decided as Johnny wound them back towards civilization.

# SNAKE OIL

**SINCLAIR'S FIRST MEETING** with Mayor Bellman came sooner than expected, as the suave leader of Hollow Hills was already waiting for Johnny and Sinclair at the station when they came in. The man was dressed to a T, wearing a tailored suit with his hair slicked away from his forehead and cuff links that glistened whenever his wrists moved. He smiled at Johnny, shaking his head and laughing even though nobody had said anything yet.

Sinclair hated the man instantly.

"Sheriff, good to see you this morning," the mayor greeted Johnny as his chuckling died down. He stepped to the side and waved his hand towards the rest of the office as if inviting Johnny into his own Sheriff's Station. "How's the town looking this morning? Still standing? Catch any criminals yet?"

"Nope," Johnny murmured, trying to match the mayor's smile, while his eyes betrayed his true feelings about the mayor.

Exhaustion.

Annoyance.

But if the Mayor noticed the look he didn't let it show as he turned his attention to Sinclair and gave a big thumbs up.

"Well, that's great. Good to hear that were in tip-top shape. And you! You must be the new Deputy I've heard so much about."

Sinclair didn't respond. He didn't believe in playing games of politeness. The mayor's cheap, fabricated facade was borderline painful to look at. For a moment, Sinclair considered letting his hangover get the better of him. He imagined vomiting all over the Mayor's fancy suit. The daydream tricked a smile over Sinclair's lips and the mayor mistook it for some sign of approval.

"See? There's a smile. Nobody can stay sour around ol' Mayor Bellman!"

The Mayor strode boldly forward and clamped a hand on Sinclair's shoulder like they were old friends and Sinclair shot a look towards Johnny to save him. But Johnny just shook his head slightly. This was just the way the mayor was. You just had to roll with it. Sinclair groaned.

"Well I don't want to keep you too long," the Mayor said, hand still holding tight to Sinclair like he was holding him still. "But it's fantastic to make your acquaintance. If there's anything you need, you just let me know."

The mayor's hand squeezed a little tighter.

"*Anything* you need. You let *me* know," he reiterated, his inflection leaving his intentions about as subtle as a grenade launcher. He glanced at Johnny whose eyes had dropped to the floor. He studied his shoelaces innocently, his face stoic and unreadable.

Sinclair lowered his shoulder and backed away from the politician's grip.

"Yup. Uh-huh. Sure," Sinclair muttered, eyes locked on Bellman's. "If I didn't know any better, Mayor, I'd say you were coming onto me," Sinclair tried to joke. Bellman smiled but didn't take the bait. Avoided addressing the accusation or the innuendo. Instead he spun on his heel and gave a curt, casual wave of his hand.

"Good luck keeping the town safe today, boys. I know Hollow Hills is in good hands. Good, capable hands. Be seeing you."

The departure felt abrupt, but Sinclair didn't mind. The faster that politician got away from Sinclair, the better. He turned back to face Johnny, to ask him what the hell that had been about, but Johnny was scowling now that the Mayor had departed, eyes shooting daggers through the window, into the man's back as he sauntered down the street towards his Benz.

"So. Is that guy as much of a douche canoe as he seems on first impression?"

"You have no idea," Johnny nodded, and he turned his focus back towards his partner again. Sinclair thought he saw something sad and introspective in Johnny's eyes, but instead of probing, Sinclair looked back outside and followed the mayor farther and farther down the road, the tension from the room leaving along with him. After watching Bellman back his car onto Main Street, Sinclair finally felt like he could breathe again, the scent of 'creep' having dissipated from the air around him. For the first time, he took a good look at the inside of the station.

He wasn't impressed.

Johnny caught his gaze and, collecting himself, waved a hand for Sinclair to follow him along the grand tour. The pair of them spent the next half hour wandering around the station getting the lay of the land. Johnny started with 'The Watchtower:' a mostly-glass-walled office in the back right corner of the building where Johnny could keep his eyes on everything happening with his officers and everything happening in the holding cell. His cube of modern architecture stood out like a bruise among 'rustic' aesthetic that dominated the rest of the station.

Next, they made their way down to the evidence locker which had been tucked in the basement and stuffed with tens, maybe hundreds of old cardboard boxes lining rows upon rows of cheap metal shelving units. Johnny told Sinclair about the way it was all *supposed* to be labeled and organized, but a quick scan of the boxes proved that the procedures were more of a suggestion than a rule. Johnny muttered something about making Cleese sort the boxes out tomorrow, but the Sheriff's tone already sounded bored of the task; as if he knew Cleese wouldn't actually do any of the work he assigned.

The pair went back upstairs, to the main office, and Johnny showed Sinclair an old desk and a rolling chair held together by duct tape. A brand new, shiny name plate sat atop the otherwise ramshackle desk along with a poorly ironed uniform, a set of keys, and a handgun with a worn leather holster.

"Mine?" Sinclair asked, nodding to where his name was engraved on the nameplate.

"Yours," Johnny confirmed as if it wasn't obvious. "Uniform won't fit great, probably. It's the old sheriff's cut from three years ago. XL instead of L, but we've got some larges ordered and on the way for you. Try not to get those too dirty in the meantime. If you do, there's some Mediums in the closet near the showers that Cleese wears, wiry little bastard. You could probably squeeze into them in a pinch, but the XLs are gonna be a hell of a lot more comfortable I'm thinking."

Sinclair nodded and fiddled with the cuff of the shirt.

"There a reason my desk is as far away from your office as possible?"

Johnny nodded and tapped his gun absent-mindedly.

"Crossfire approach. I can watch what's going on from my glass watchtower, you can watch everybody from the opposite side. Nobody's backs ever turned to both of us at once. Then there's a second set of keys to everything- the evidence lockers, the drunk tank, even the damn truck in case I need you to go pick up a perp. Mi casa es su casa."

Sinclair poked the keys and eyed the gun, looking around the space. It was so much smaller than Charlotte, but somehow held the same air of secrets and distrust, as if the whispers of corruption had caught in the cobwebs in the corners.

"What are we cross firing? Expecting a bunch of perps to be staging jail breaks when we bring in their buddies or something?"

Johnny turned towards the other two desks with O'Hare and Cleese inscribed on their nameplates. He didn't answer Sinclair directly, but his gaze highlighted his concerns well enough.

"Or something . . . " he said softly.

Sinclair nodded and poked at the stuff on his desk.

"I don't want the gun," he told his boss.

"I knew you wouldn't. Not your style. But put it on just in case. You never draw the damn thing, that's fine by me, but have it with you. You never know when a dog's gonna get rabies and our jobs'll come down to putting the mutt down or watching some kid get mauled."

Sinclair hesitated, his hand hovering over the desk for a moment before he plucked all the items from the desk and put them in a worn down 'Hollow Hills Sheriff's Department' duffel bag which was on the floor nearby. He zipped the black bag up, frowned, turned back to his old friend and asked the question that had been nagging him.

"So what's the mayor got to hide, then?" Sinclair decided to pry. "Talking to me like that, right in front of you seems like a bold play. Nobody takes a risk like that unless there's something big at stake. Or unless I'm wrong about how risky that was, for him to try to bribe me in front of you . . . " Sinclair cocked an eyebrow at Johnny, asking him about his relationship with the potentially-corrupt-mayor without really asking him.

"I hear you, man. Nah, I'm not in his pocket or anything." Johnny let the claim sit in the air for a moment, but Sinclair didn't push him on it. This was his friend. His boss. He had to trust him or else the move out here would have been entirely pointless.

"But that snake knows how to play the game, I'll give that to him. You'll get used to him. He's always present, always approaching people with ninety percent of promises dangled about, suggested but not defined, just to see who he can pull into his corner. I've never heard him say or do anything overtly illegal, but just . . . yeah. Keep your guard up. He's an odd duck."

"No clue what he's hiding?"

"I'm not totally convinced he *is* hiding anything. It might just be a weird politician thing. Collecting as many chips as possible in case he needs them later. That sort of a deal. But I've never been sure. It's part of why I brought you up here. I don't know these people. I can't trust these people. Not totally. Everything seems so squeaky clean on the surface, but then you meet people like the Mayor, like Rochester, and it just feels like there's more to the story, you know?"

Sinclair nodded in understanding.

"Watch them from both sides. Crossfire approach. Got it. I'm with you."

"Cool. Thanks, man. Fingers crossed we keep our eyes peeled for a decade, bust something ridiculous as innocuous as an illegal peacock breeding ring, then retire into the sunset having gone beyond the call of duty."

Sinclair furrowed his brow.

"Peacock breeding ring? That's a weirdly specific thing to just come up with."

"Oh my god, I haven't told you about the Davis family yet, have I? Hold your dick, this one's great."

Johnny spent the next couple of hours filling Sinclair in on more and more of the town gossip until it was finally lunch time. The pair left the station together to stop by Mama Jeans for a pair of hoagies before they drove out to the peacock farm on the edge of town. Sinclair had to see that for himself. The absurdity of Hollow Hills' stories dulled the threat that the Mayor had posed, and Sinclair was almost able to forget the paranoid feeling he'd had in his gut the whole time that Bellman spoke to him. The feeling that promised Sinclair something really was wrong around here, even if Johnny didn't see it yet. Even if Johnny was privy to it.

# BIRDS OF PREY

JOHNNY HADN'T BEEN kidding. There was a goddamn peacock farm.

Sinclair pressed his back against the squad car and held his lunch as high as possible over head as one of the peacocks flapped its brilliantly colored feathers and clacked its beak in the air, trying to reach the bread.

Johnny was a few steps away laughing his ass off, offering no help as Mr. Davis descended his porch steps, hollering "Shoo!" at the top of his lungs. But the bird paid him no attention.

The peacock squawked, a high-pitched piercing sound that reminded Sinclair more of the velociraptors from Jurassic Park than the sound any real bird would have made.

There was a clacking sound on the car behind Sinclair and the sandwich jerked free from his hands. A second peacock had mounted Johnny's truck, giving it just enough height to reach Sinclair's held-aloft lunch.

"Son of a bitch!"

"Hah! Them's some smart-ass birds right there. Learned to work together a few years ago. Thems don't do it too often, but when there's food on the line you best watch your ass! But really. Watch your ass. They don't take too kindly to grown ups. Mostly just seem to get along with the kids, and I suspect its cause the kids sneak 'em table scraps." Mr. Davis said, coming to a stop beside Johnny and watching as two more peacocks descended on the sandwich formerly known as Sinclair's.

"We'll get you another sandwich on the way home, bud. Why do you think I ate mine in the car?"

"I thought it was because you were hungry!" Sinclair shouted, flustered and not controlling his volume.

Another peacock strutted out of the nearby bushes, and now

suddenly there were five peacocks all surrounding the sandwich, pecking away for their portion of the kill.

Sinclair moved slowly past the flock, nervous that moving too fast might agitate them, get the birds to come after him instead of the salami and Swiss cheese they had already claimed.

"So there's really peacocks out here?"

"Yeah!"

" . . . Why? . . . " Sinclair couldn't help but ask.

"Makes a crap ton of money!" Mr. Davis offered and, glancing around, Sinclair assumed the man must have been right. The Davis house was enormous. Three stories high with a barn out back. It was more than Sinclair could have ever afforded on two of his own salaries.

Mr. Davis himself was dressed well, a neatly pressed button-down shirt tucked into a pair of unblemished dress pants with a pair of hundred-dollar loafers.

"Maybe I should get into this business, huh?"

"Don't be modest, honey!" a new lady, Mrs. Davis presumably, said as she emerged and walked over from behind the barn, two more peacocks following at her sides like a pair of dogs. "All this didn't come from the damn peacocks, though they don't hurt. Mikey here works six days a week down at the Gattis Mill also. These peacocks are more like a fun hobby."

"A fun, lucrative hobby," Mikey Davis added. "You have any interest in buying a couple? I'll sell 'em to you at a bargain. Call it a 'Welcome To Town' deal," Mr. Davis offered, his eyes glittering at the prospect of a sale.

Beside Mikey, Johnny was having a hard time containing his laughter as he shook his head 'No' as vigorously as possible.

Sinclair glanced again towards the raptors which were tearing his sandwich apart.

"Yeah, no. Gonna pass on that one," he said as he stepped forward. "Name's Sinclair by the way. Sinclair Redford. Sounds like you've gathered I'm new in town."

"Oh, yeah, yeah. Word's been gettin' around about you already. Word gets around this town pretty fast whenever something new happens. Yup, Betty just called up Sherlene this morning and told her she saw you at the tavern last night drinkin' up a storm."

"I wouldn't say I was drinking up a storm . . . "

"Yeah. Way she tells it, you might be able to give Hank Truman a run for his money at the Oktoberfest Games next year!"

"I don't know what that is. And no, I don't really drink that much."

"Don't be modest, son. *Somebody* needs to knock Hank off his throne. Bastard's getting too cozy up there."

Sinclair shot Johnny a 'help me' sort of a look and Johnny just smiled back at him.

"Well okay then, maybe we'll see what I can do next month, huh?" Sinclair offered, hoping that might get him out of the conversation. He didn't like this. Mikey was acting way too familiar with him, like they were friends. It made Sinclair uncomfortable. God, next thing he knew the man might try to hug him or something.

"So yeah. Johnny just wanted to show me the peacock farm and, um, well, now I guess I've seen them, so we might want to get a move on. Stuff in the town to attend to, right Johnny?"

"Nah. Town's probably fine," Johnny said and very discreetly showed Sinclair his middle finger. He was enjoying watching Sinclair squirm.

"Can't leave yet! You just got here and Sherlene made some apple pies just a bit ago. I'll bet they're still warm!"

Mrs. Davis nodded and glanced back towards their house.

"Oughta be just about perfect eatin' temperature by now. Let me just get Barker and the boys in here and we'll tucker in," Sherlene Davis said and she cocked her head to the side, looking over her shoulder towards the woods before she let out one of the most ungodly hollers Sinclair had ever heard.

"BARKER! BAKER! CARL! CAL! YOU GET YOUR ASSES IN HERE, WE'RE EATIN PIES!"

Sinclair nearly leapt from his shoes. How had such a small lady made so much noise? Even the peacocks paused their destruction of Sinclair's sandwich to look up and hiss their disdain at her.

There was a rustling of bushes and a trio of new peacocks charged into the driveway followed by four young kids brandishing sticks, waving them at the backs of the birds' tucked-back tails and at each other in equal measure.

"Pie, pie, pie," they were chanting, but when they saw the Sheriff's car and Johnny standing there, they all skidded to a halt. The tallest kid lowered something that looked like a dog whistle from his lips. The peacocks glanced towards him, glanced at the whistle, and then scattered, wandering away from the trio of children to clack their beaks at the peacocks which had stolen Sinclair's sandwich.

The kids dropped their sticks and tried to shrink to become as small as possible, suddenly on their best behavior and trying to side-step towards their parents.

"Howdy, kiddos," Johnny said, smiling at them all.

"Officer," the tallest kid with red hair responded.

"Y'all been on your best behavior recently?"

"Yes sir. Of course sir. Haven't been doing nothing wrong."

"No more breaking the windows of that abandoned house?"

"Nope," the tall kid said in the least convincing way possible.

"Or tearing up old lady Howell's garden?"

"Nuh-uh. We've just been playing here. Tending our birds. Doing our chores and our homeworks."

The smallest kid slapped the taller kid in the back and spoke up for the first time, "He knows we don't do our homeworks. He talks to Mrs. Johnson, remember?"

"Oh yeah. No homeworks. But we've been tending the birds and not breaking any more windows, no sir," the tall kid tried to salvage the lie.

Johnny just shook his head and looked up at the kids' mother.

Sherlene Davis nodded her head.

"They've been good here, Officer. And you know I'd wear their hides out myself if they weren't."

Johnny nodded again.

"What's that?" Sinclair asked the tallest boy, pointing towards the whistle in his hands.

The kid looked at the device.

"Why? Its not illegal."

"What? No. Of course not. I just want to-"

"-You have to have a warrant if you want to search my things. I knows that. I knows my rights."

"Jesus, kid. I'm just trying to ask a question."

"That there's his peacock whistle," Mrs. Davis interjected before her son could be any more obstinate. "Like a dog whistle. But for peacocks. Barker made it himself, didn't you, Barker?"

Barker didn't answer. Just stared back at Sinclair as if daring him to try to confiscate it.

"Go on. Show him what it does. Then we'll get that pie."

Barker raised the whistle to his lips begrudgingly, gave it a quick, short, puff that was inaudible to Sinclair, but freaked the peacocks right the hell out. Each one craned their necks around to look at their little master. Another peacock, unseen until now, burst up onto the Davis family's roof, emerging from some unseen backyard. Sinclair could imagine all of them screaming about food, the same image of a sandwich burned to their front of their minds like the seagulls from Finding Nemo.

Mine?

One of the peacocks screeched, a sudden, high-pitched dinosaur-like sound which made Sinclair jump halfway out of his skin.

He really wasn't a fan of these damn birds.

Barker Davis laughed at Sinclair.

"Well it was good to see y'all again, but Sinclair might have actually been right. Oughta go check back into town after all. Thanks for letting the newbie meet your birds like that, and Barker you enjoy your pie. You've earned it for keepin' your nose clean this past month I suppose.

Mr. Davis smiled at that and nodded, like he was proud of his kid for not pissing off the Sheriff for 'so long.'

"Oh yes sir, the kiddos have turned over a new leaf, haven't you boys?"

All four of the kids' heads bobbed up and down in unison, but they wouldn't meet Sinclair or Johnny's eyes. Pack of liars, Sinclair knew, but he bit his tongue. He just wanted to get out of here, away from the birds who had finished his sandwich by now and which were turning away from Barker, back towards him as they expected more.

Holy shit, he really hated peacocks, it turned out.

Johnny tipped his hat in the family's direction and, shooing a couple of the birds out of his path, he made his way back to the driver's side door.

"Nice to meet y'all," Sinclair said with a little wave. He tried to think of some compliment to say about the peacocks, but came up with nothing. Stupid hobby. Stupid animals. Terrible, angry, sharp beaks. Sinclair didn't really listen to the Davis family's responses as he swung his door open and slipped back inside before the beasts could approach him again.

Johnny fired up the engine and began to back the car around, moving slowly so he didn't run over any of the birds which were scattering in all directions. He was laughing about Sinclair and waving over the dash at the family. The kids were already gone, racing towards the house to get their promised slices of pie.

"They seem . . . nice?" Sinclair tried to be polite.

"Huh? Oh, hell no. That family sucks. Peacocks are funny shit, but those kids are monsters. Bet you ten bucks one of them's going to be in the back of this cruiser between now and those Oktoberfest Games which you're gonna win now, huh?"

Sinclair shook his head and looked down at his knees.

"I'm not doing that,"

"Sure you are. You told Sherlene you'd do it, which means you've basically told Betty that you'd do it, which means you've practically told Howie Short that you'd do it, and he's in charge of the whole thing. Guy's probably writing your name down on the list already. News travels fast around here, and nobody ever forgets a damned thing."

The two of them talked about the Octoberfest celebrations and the peacocks and the Davis family all the way back to town. The kids were hooligans. Vandals and nuisances of the highest degree, and Johnny would have been amazed if he knew how quickly he was going to lose his ten dollar bet with Sinclair.

# DARKNESS FALLS

**THE NIGHT BEFORE** Hollow Hills' collapse began, Johnny slept restlessly. He kept waking up thinking he was on fire, sweating through his sheets despite the cool summer air and his open windows. He chalked it up to a fever. He never usually got sick, but maybe five years without so much as a cold just meant that he was "due". He took some ibuprofen and shivered under an extra layer of covers until the sun rose.

Sinclair had another run-in with the dead. This time his son. Two legs stretched from beneath his bed on one side while a little voice cried for help from the opposite end; an impossible stretch of space separating the two halves of Max from each other. Up above, Sinclair sweat through his mattress, too afraid and too ashamed to climb down to look under the bed frame. He knew he should go to his boy. He knew he should try to save him. He knew that was his duty as a father. The fact that he didn't move ate away at what remained of his soul.

All up and down Hollow Hills, dogs barked. Cats hissed at shadows. Flowers wilted and died for no apparent reason.

Something was coming, and nobody saw what it was besides Barker Davis.

About that same hour as Sinclair clenched his eyes firmly shut, the Davis kids mounted their bikes and snuck out of their house; their slices of pie fully digested; the peacocks fed and watered for the night. The children rode with mischief on their minds, and they glid silently all the way past the station, through the downtown area, and up past the creepy doll-infested tree that marked the edge of the Rochester property.

# RED RUM

JOHNNY TURNED THE truck onto Maple Street slowly, still not fully awake. It was going to be the last day he picked Sinclair up for work. That bum was gonna have to fix his damned car soon. Maybe get a bike from Jeffrey's shop, if nothing else. Didn't matter. Sinclair had a whole weekend to figure out his transportation options, but he wasn't going to lean on Johnny like this anymore. No sir.

Johnny tapped the wheel, waiting for a red light to turn green, sitting patiently despite the fact that no traffic ever crossed Maple Street. Never. He could have run the light and been fine. Shaved what felt like another 30 minutes off of this commute.

But no.

He was the Sherriff. He had an image to uphold.

Johnny rolled his eyes, playing ping-pong with his thoughts while he waited.

Who was Johnny kidding? Sinclair wasn't going to get his shit together over the weekend. He was going to call Johnny first thing Monday morning to see if he could get a lift and yeah, Johnny was gonna come pick him up again. That's what friends were for. But driving all the way across town just to drive all the way back to the station was tedious, especially with these damned time-locked streetlights.

Also, from a less selfish standpoint, Johnny told himself that he really just wanted his friend to snap out of his funk. To start participating in things like driving a car again. Getting to work on his own. Being self-sufficient. Maybe it was still too soon for that. Johnny knew Sinclair's world got absolutely fucking rocked back in Charlotte, and Johnny was trying his best to be sensitive to that.

But damn.

If the peacocks yesterday hadn't jostled some pep into Sinclair's step, then Johnny was plumb out of ideas.

He racked his brain, trying to think of what else the town had to offer that might excite his friend. Get him plugged back into the world again.

The light turned green and Johnny turned left onto Birch Street, building up just the slightest bit of speed before slamming on his brakes and grinding the truck back to a halt.

Dead in front of Johnny, a child stood in the center of the street, covered head to foot with blood. Every inch of the boy was coated crimson except for two terrified white eyes which darted about, wincing at every owl call and every sputter of Johnny's truck's engine.

It was hard to recognize the kid at first, through his matted hair, with his usual tan skin stained red and still dripping.

But those eyes.

Barker Davis.

"No shit," Johnny shouted, jumping from his truck and barely remembering to put the vehicle in park. What was he doing all the way out here?

"Kid, hey kid!" Johnny called as he stumbled up the asphalt, his feet forgetting how to function in the shock of the moment.

Barker startled, his head teetering back and forth like it was too heavy for his neck to support, and Johnny scanned the kid up and down, looking for the source of blood as he approached.

Something was wrong here.

No.

A *lot* was wrong here. He wanted to scoop the kid up, to get him back to the safety of his truck, but Johnny recognized that charging up to a traumatized child and grabbing them by the shoulders was probably the wrong move. Barker, this kid who was constantly climbing up the walls and talking a mile a minute, was dead silent, and a fragile peace hung in the air.

Johnny slowed to a halt about five steps from the boy. He had to be careful not to shatter that tension. There was no telling what the panicked kid might do. Run. Attack. Die of fright. Johnny tried to present himself as tender as possible as he lowered himself down to one knee.

"Kid?" Johnny whispered. "I need you to talk to me."

Johnny kept his tone hushed and scanned to his left and his right to see if anybody else was around who could help him. But there was nobody. Mayor Bellman's tall hedges stood to his right, watching the proceedings apathetically. No other cars were approaching. It was too early in the morning for traffic to be at full steam yet, and this was a random-ass back road anyhow.

Johnny was going in alone here.

"Kid. I need you to talk to me, kid. What's the deal with all the . . . um . . . red on you?" Johnny didn't think saying *blood* out loud was the right call. The kid seemed to be on pins and needles. Drawing his attention back to the fact that he was covered in blood would be tactless, to say the least. Holy hell, what was going on here?

The blood didn't seem like it was Barker's. At least, there weren't any wounds that Johnny could see. And that much blood, the wound would surely be visible, wouldn't it? Right?

Barker held his peacock bird whistle thing in his hands, clutching it like a life preserver. But the bird was nowhere to be seen. Could this have been the peacocks doing? Had Barker and his brothers finally smacked their birds with sticks one too many times? Where were Barker's brothers? So much was wrong with this scene that Johnny couldn't process it all at once.

Johnny tracked the kids' bloody footsteps back away from him, up the road towards . . . towards . . . shitsticks, that was the direction of the Rochester House. What had Barker been doing back that way?

Johnny drew in a long, deep breath and let it out slowly, trying to stay focused on the kid.

One step at a time.

Collect the kid.

Get him safe.

*Then* figure out what the hell happened.

"Barker," Johnny said, and the kids' eyes finally focused, just a bit, at the sound of his name. "I've got a towel in the back of my truck. I'm gonna get in to grab it, and I'm gonna wrap you up, and I'm gonna get you back to the station. We'll call your mama on the way and get her to meet us there. That sound good? Get you a shower at the station to wash the . . . ."

Again, Johnny stopped himself from saying blood. Maybe, somehow, the kid didn't know what he was covered in. Maybe, somehow, his innocent mind had just blocked all this out. No need to call attention to the carnage. Jesus, that was so much blood. Keep the kid calm, though. Keep the kid calm. Keep the kid calm and get him safe.

" . . . to wash up . . . and then we'll get your mama, and we'll get a biscuit from Mama Jean's for you. Huh? How about that?" Johnny opened his driver's door back up as he spoke, fumbled around for the towel he had mentioned, then reapproached the child slowly.

"Muffer," it sounded like Barker whispered.

"What was that? "Johnny asked and the kid fell forward. Smeared blood all over the Sheriff's uniform as he threw his arms around Johnny, hugging him tight.

Johnny hugged the kid back, trying to project comfort and protection through the embrace.

"Mur . . . mur . . . murderer." Barker finally managed to whisper in Johnny's ear. It was like two faucets had been turned. Tears gushed down the child's face and he collapsed, limp in Johnny's arms as the Sheriff rose, swaddling the kid in the towel and placing him gently, but quickly, into the passenger seat of his truck.

"Where's your brothers, Barker?" Johnny asked as he clicked the passenger seat's buckle into place.

Barker didn't respond.

Johnny rushed to the driver's seat and floored it the rest of the way to Sinclair's place. He slammed on the horn without thinking about it and Barker jumped a mile high in the seat next to him.

"Shit, sorry kid. SINCLAIR GET YOUR ASS OUT HERE!"

On cue, Sinclair's front door opened. The newly deputized shuffled down the walk slowly, casually wandering towards his boss's truck and casting a sideways glance at his own car before noticing the blood-soaked mess in the passenger seat.

"You're in the bed today," Johnny offered by way of explanation. "Come on. We've gotta get to the station now!"

And for the first time since Sinclair had arrived in town, Johnny saw the man hustle into action.

# A SUSPECT. A CLUE.

**AN HOUR LATER,** just about everybody in the station was screaming.

Mr. and Mrs. Davis had arrived and started shouting accusations at each officer in the department, howling that they should have done more to protect their baby boy. Cleese and O'Hare were shouting back, angry that they had been called in to work on their day off. Johnny was shouting back at them, gesturing to the blood-soaked child sitting in his office, and asking them what their definition of an emergency was. Literally the only person who wasn't at the top of their lungs, besides Sinclair, was Barker.

Sinclair hadn't heard the kid utter a sound, despite all the Sheriff's questioning.

"Who did this to you, Barker?"

"What happened, Barker?"

"Where are your brothers, Barker?"

It was like all the questions fell on deaf ears. The kid just stared straight ahead, dead-eyed like a fish, until Johnny gave up on the questions and left Sinclair in charge.

The Davis parents confirmed the other Davis kids were back home, safe, but confused. So that was a small relief. But still, it left Johnny and Sinclair with the question of whose blood covered Barker.

"If you can get him to say Rochester's name, then we go in guns blazing with a warrant. If not, we can do a house call under reasonable suspicion, but that's about it. Keep working on the kid. Get him to talk. But do it gently. I'll try to handle the parents," Johnny had told Sinclair, after pulling him to the side. "Whole thing is FUBAR, but we've gotta piece all this together before word gets out to the rest of town. I've kept Sherlene away from the phones for about as long as I can, but she's gonna start the rumor mill churning sooner rather than later, and when it does, we'll need some official story to run with so we don't just look like a bunch of assholes."

Sinclair had nodded and returned to Johnny's office, where the kid was sitting, wrapped in his blanket. He had tried to small talk the kid into feeling comfortable with him, but it didn't seem to be working.

"Peacocks didn't do this to you, did they?"

It was a joke. A bad joke, but one that should have cracked a smile from the kid, right? It would have gotten a smile from Max.

Barker Davis' eyes went a little wider, but he just kept staring at the nothingness in front of him. No response.

Sinclair checked the kids' pulse as he listened to Johnny argue with the parents about something in the next room over. Barker's heart was beating like a jackhammer.

"Tell you what, kid. You don't seem to want to talk so maybe let's try something else. Let's just do visual cues, huh? I'll show you some pictures. You see the guy that did this to you, then you just flinch a little bit. Or blink a bunch. You know? Whatever suits you?"

It was a dumb idea. But what the hell, Sinclair was stuck in this room with the kid whether he had good ideas or bad ideas. This would help pass the time at least.

Sinclair pulled out his cell phone, tabbed past all his CNN APP updates, and found the Safari Explorer.

"Mikey Davis. Peacocks" he typed into the search bar. Sure enough, the Davis Domestic Peacocks business page came up as one of the first results, and there was the kid's dad, standing between two full-colored birds. Sinclair showed the picture to the kid.

"This who did it?"

Barker's thousand-yard stare remained.

"Nah. Didn't think so. You can usually tell when it's the dad involved. Still had to check."

It was a good control variable. No reaction at all to the dad. So, if there was a reaction to something else, Sinclair would know the kid wasn't just jumping at ghosts.

Sinclair opened a new search tab in his browser.

"Rochester. Toy Maker. Hollow Hills," Sinclair typed as much information as he could remember into the search engine. Google came up with an old news article with a grainy picture; probably from the 90s based on the man's mop-like hair and baggy, plaid clothes. Sinclair had never seen Rochester before, but sure. This must be the right guy. In the picture, he stood in front of the now-defunct Toy Store from downtown, grinning from ear to ear, hugging a crowd of kids close up against him.

'Toy Maker in Rural Town Gives Away Half of Inventory for Holidays,' the title read. That gave Sinclair a pause. Seemed like an awfully charitable thing for a crazed, doll-hanging, blood spraying, potential murderer to do.

Oh well.

Sometimes it was the people who you least expected.

In Charlotte, Sinclair had seen the worst of the worst. Pedophiles especially tended to catch him off guard. Was he hugging those kids a little too close in the picture?

Sinclair spun the phone around to show Barker.

This time, the reaction was immediate, and so jarring it almost shocked Sinclair out of his own chair. The kid screamed like he was being stabbed, his eyes suddenly focusing and dilating as he threw his hands up for protection, knocking the phone free from Sinclair's grip.

At the noise, the door flew open, and Johnny burst back into his Watchtower office, followed up the steps by the Davis adults.

"The hell did you do to . . . " Johnny's voice trailed off.

He saw the picture of Rochester on Sinclair's phone.

He saw the fresh tears streaming down the victim's eyes.

"Cleese! Warrant! Now!" Johnny shouted over his shoulder as he stepped aside to let Barker's parents' past. "Get to the truck. I'll meet you there with the papers in a minute."

"Don't we need to get him to say-"

"No. Shut up. This is good enough for hand grenades and horseshoes. Now get a move on, that shithead could be halfway to California by now. He's gotta know we'll be after his ass."

Sinclair rose from his chair, collected his phone from the ground, and cast a sad look towards the panicking kid who was being smothered by his parents.

"Sorry, Barker," he said.

He felt bad for freaking the kid out. But that was the job sometimes, wasn't it? The bad guys didn't play fair so neither could he. He made his way out the front of the station and did what he had been told, buckling himself into the still-blood-stained passenger seat and waiting for Johnny to rush out to join him, warrant still hot from the printer.

# MASTER OF PUPPETS

**JOHNNY'S TRUCK TORE** up the half-mud, half-gravel drive to Rochester House at nearly fifty miles an hour. Branches from the surrounding woods slapped the side of his car, and the ruts in the old, weathered drive jostled them back and forth. The dolls feet tap against the truck's roof as they drive under the lynching tree, and Sinclair sucks in a breath while maintaining a firm grip on the "Oh Shit" handle over the passenger seat. His side of the truck still smells of the kids' blood, and Johnny looks like he is about to erupt with excitement. Something was happening in his town, his smile said. Something was *finally* happening.

"We're coming up here to cuff the guy, Johnny. Remember that," Sinclair said. And Johnny glances over at his friend, some of the color returning to his knuckles, gripping the steering wheel.

"I know. I know. I'm just gonna be fucking off the handle if we missed our chance to bring this asshole in. What he did to that kid . . . "

"We don't know that was him."

"But based on the kids' reaction?"

"We don't know what he did."

"The kid was covered in blood!"

"We've got a warrant, but no evidence. Assumptions, but no story. Just breathe, Johnny. Breathe. It'll come together."

And Johnny did.

Long, slow breaths.

He nodded, seeming to have his shit back together for the moment, but Sinclair's nerves were on red alert now. He hadn't seen Johnny this heated since they fired him back in Charlotte.

Their truck bucked to its right, hard, and it was a miracle they didn't lose a tire in the pothole Johnny flew over. The vehicle jerked into, then out of, a bush, found the driveway again, and wavered its way to the top of a slight hill.

# STRING THEM UP

The Rochester House revealed itself to them like a monster rising from the Earth, its broken siding and feral grounds recalling Sinclair's own house with alarming similarity. Johnny's truck slid to a stop just a few short feet from the front porch and the driver's side door burst open before the engine was even off.

"Rochester! Sheriff's Department! We need you to come out with your hands up!" Johnny shouted as he moved, taking the steps to the porch two at a time, all proper procedures be damned.

Sinclair leapt from his seat also, but instead of rushing towards the door to the house, like Johnny was, Sinclair instead tried to head off his friend.

"Johnny, Johnny, Johnny, chill."

"What?"

Sinclair pointed towards a dilapidated barn, set a short way behind the house. Poking out from around the corner was a truck-old, but looking fresh enough that it probably still ran.

"That his truck?" Sinclair asked.

Johnny tore his eyes away from the front door and followed Sinclair's finger towards the truck.

"Yup," Johnny confirmed.

"So, if his truck's here, then he's probably here still too?"

Johnny paused, then muttered "Yup," again, his voice more level now, the eagerness from his eyes abated at least slightly.

"Well then, he hasn't flown the coop. He's probably here. Now let's slow down and lets not go barreling into this like a bunch of assholes that want to get stripped of their badges."

It took a second, but Johnny eventually nodded again.

"Yeah. Yep. Alright. You're right. Sin, you go take the back door. Make sure he doesn't bolt for it if he's inside. I'll knock on the front all polite-like. We give him two chances, then we go in."

Sinclair stared at his chief hard for a minute, making sure his friend actually had his head screwed on straight. It seemed like he did. The vein in his temple had stopped bulging out at the very least, and his teeth weren't clenched like they had been in the truck.

Sinclair huffed and made his way towards the back door like he'd been told. As he walked, he took the time to really assess his surroundings.

Just like the tree in the front, dolls of all shapes and sizes littered the property, arranged like the whole place was some oversized playset. Some dolls sat on swings. Others were laid out on blankets like they were having a picnic. Still more had their arms propped and slung up, suspended from trees as puppets engaged in their various activities, holding butterfly nets, climbing ladders.

These dolls weren't mutilated the way that the dolls on the gallows tree had been, though. None of them were in *pristine* condition, but there was a care to the way they had all been set up and arranged. Farther away, life-sized, mannequin-ish fuckers were set up in the woods, the faces painted on them showcasing happiness and sadness like tragedy masks at the theater. Sinclair stared at these for an extra second to make sure none of the mannequins moved; to make sure none were actually Rochester staking out his own property to see what the Sheriff would do. But the mannequins were impassive.

It creeped Sinclair the hell right out.

Behind him, Johnny was already knocking on the front door.

"Hollow Hills Sheriff's Department. Gregory Rochester, you need to come out with your hands up. We have a warrant to search the premises."

Sinclair reached the back door, planning to do little more than standing there with his arms crossed, waiting for the suspect to come racing away from Johnny's voice. But the back door was open already and the sounds of a skipping record wafted through the entryway.

Curious, Sinclair glanced again at the woods behind him, re-scanning the mannequins' faces. Had their suspect already flown the coop?

The mannequins stared back, blank expressions on their faces refusing to tattle on their creator's whereabouts and so Sinclair frowned, took a few more steps towards the back door.

Out front Johnny called out for a second time, going through his list of legally mandated disclaimers before he kicked the door down.

Sinclair's hand inched towards the gun, holstered to his hip. He didn't intend to use it, but his hand moved by habit, like a toddler reaching for their blanket. Just feeling the rough grip against his palm helped to ease Sinclair's suddenly itchy nerves as he stepped up the three rotting steps to the Rochester House and glanced inside.

There were more puppets in here. Hundreds more. The

skipping record was situated on an end table next to a couch where three puppets were propped upright, their heads turned towards the spinning machine as if they were engrossed by the same three trumpet notes warbling over and over and over and over. A vase of dead flowers had been situated over the mantle and dust motes chased each other through the beams of light which snuck through the broken windows. But what really caught Sinclair's attention, held it and refused to let him look away, was the figure of his dead wife on the landing above the staircase.

He recognized her from his nightmares; the left half of her face slumped a few inches lower than normal, her skull not sitting quite right because of the crack which separated her eye socket from her ear. Her left eye had ruptured in the fire and blood and chunks of deflated retina painted her cheek, her chin, and the front of her favorite shirt.

Yet despite all of this, she still smiled at Sinclair.

Across the main floor of the house, the front door exploded inwards as Johnny rammed it with his shoulder, splitting the wood free from its hinges.

Sinclair jumped at the sound, his attention turning away from his wife for the briefest of instances, but when he looked back, she was gone.

"Hollow Hills Sheriff's Department, Gregory come out with your- Sin, what the hell?" Johnny shouted as Sinclair bolted towards the stairs, forgetting all about his training and all procedures. The needle skipped off the record as Sinclair rushed past, bumping into the nightstand in his haste. "I thought you told me we needed to be calm!" Johnny yelled, also abandoning his shallow efforts at professionalism as he hurtled the doll-adorned couch, slid around a mannequin which had been dressed up like a 1930s farmhand looking for work.

Sinclair led the way up the stairs, Johnny just a few short steps behind him.

"Sin, slow down, we don't know what's going on in here. This could be dangerous."

The words had barely left Johnny's lips when the stairs collapsed under his feet, and the Sheriff of Hollow Hills plummeted down into whatever darkness waited beneath the moldy wood.

At the top of the stairs, Sinclair paused, torn between pursuing his dead wife and turning back to check on his living friend.

He leaned over a banister and gazed down at the black hole where Johnny had fallen. Sinclair couldn't see anything. The hole looked deep and must have fallen all the way through the first floor into the house's basement if it had one.

"Johnny! Say something."

"Fuck me," the response came up from the hole, and Johnny sounded angry, but probably not wounded. Somehow.

"You okay?" Sinclair called, but he got distracted before he could hear Johnny's response. Something was creaking on the second floor behind him.

The upper landing where Sinclair stood branched off in three different directions, and to Sinclair's left a door stood slightly ajar, sickly yellow light peeking out from around the open door's frame, beckoning Sinclair to come closer. The creaking sound was coming from inside.

"Johnny, you hang tight," Sinclair called down, lowering his voice, and hoping that Johnny could still hear him.

Sinclair's attention was fixed singularly on the door, on the sounds. Is that where his wife had gone? He shifted his weight to his toes and crept forward, trying to make as little noise as possible. The creaking grew louder and now Sinclair could hear hurried whispering, like secrets were being told to the light in the room behind the door.

The door screeched inward, its hinges howling their discontent about having to moved, as if they had remained still for years, had grown comfortable in their permanent positions.

Inside, puppets covered every conceivable surface. Each one seated carefully upright with their heads turned towards where Sinclair stood, petrified, caught off guard by their volume and their attention. It felt like a hundred tiny eyes were staring back at him, an entire auditorium worth of little faces judging him from the top of a pair of dressers, gazing down from the heights of an old wooden wardrobe, and starting him down from the bed where they had been mounded up on top of one another.

The whispering stopped immediately.

Sinclair's breath caught in his throat.

There was something else in here, too. Not just the puppets, but on the bed, a man lay, eyes closed, covered in blood. His crimson arms were wrapped around one of the dolls, its ear pulled close to the man's lips which continued to move, though the whispers had grown softer, harder to hear.

Old Man Rochester.

Sinclair grabbed his gun, ripping it free from its holster, his usual reservations be damned.

"On the ground, now!"

The man's eyes opened slowly, the blood crusted on his eyelashes stretching and cracking to let him see. His hair was shoulder-length, damp and mottled with dry blood, and Sinclair realized that beneath the layer of blood, the man was completely naked. His wardrobe of gore had stained the mattress and covers beneath him completely, and though the man turned his opened eyes towards Sinclair, he made no effort to get out of the bed, as instructed.

"So, you're Sinclair," the man rasped, his voice catching and gravelly as if his vocal chords were sticking with dried blood as well, the words dry like cement after remaining stagnant for so long.

How did he know Sinclair's name?

Sinclair squared his shoulders up with the bed, tensed his forearms and waggled the end of the gun in the man's direction again. "Get on the ground."

The man still didn't move. He just stared back at Sinclair, his eyes glassy and unfocused, like the doll's sitting next to him.

Behind Sinclair there was a commotion, and the deputy heard Johnny working his way around the hole in the staircase.

"Shit, Sinclair. Seriously. You've gotta get to the basement there's a goddamn-" Johnny stopped when he saw Old Man Rochester, raised the gun which he already had drawn and leveled it at the man, his head whipping around and taking stock of the rest of the room.

No threats besides the naked man in the bed. Only puppets.

"Gregory Rochester, we are hereby placing you under arrest," Johnny said as he panned around, approaching the back of the bed while leaving Sinclair's sight lines clear. Johnny started rattling off Mr. Rochester's Miranda Rights as he worked a zip tie around the man's wrists.

Rochester never resisted; never made any move until Johnny pulled him up, off the bed.

With the suspect cuffed, Sinclair finally re-holstered his weapon. He kept eye contact with Rochester though. There was something in the old man's eyes that unsettled Sinclair. Behind the dull luster of whatever drugs the man was on, Sinclair imagined he could sense a familiarity in the man's eyes. He looked at Sinclair the way that he would look at an old friend after a long absence; the way Sinclair imagined he had looked at Johnny when he first showed up in town.

"How do you know me?" Sinclair repeated, quietly, as Johnny led the blood-covered toymaker past him, back into the hall, towards the stairs.

"All in good time, boy-o." Rochester whispered, and he winked as he passed. Sinclair was left alone in the room with all the puppets, glancing from the blood-stained bed, back at all the dolls whose eyes stared at the spot on the bed where their creator had lain, whispering to them in the early morning light.

Sinclair didn't notice that; the changing of their head positions. He left the room, oblivious, and shut the door carefully, quietly, behind him.

"We'll get him back to the station and then come back here for a full sweep. I've gotta stitch up this hole in my side," Johnny called over his shoulder as he maneuvered their suspect past the hole in the steps. Sinclair noticed for the first time a red stain covering the left side of his boss's torso, the way Johnny's shirt had been torn when he fell through the stairs.

"You see anything in the basement while you were down there?"

"Not a thing. Just a dark as shit basement. Like I said, we'll double back."

Johnny threw a distrusting look at Rochester who was being suspiciously calm for a man in the process of being arrested.

Sinclair huffed and started making his way down the steps as well, ignoring the whispers which started up again in the room behind him.

# BREACHING THE CASTLE WALLS

**WHILE SINCLAIR AND JOHNNY** were away, the station was overrun. It looked like the whole town was crowded around the front doors, standing on their tiptoes, eyes strained to try to get a glimpse of Barker and his family.

Johnny slammed on the horn and pulled into his parking spot intentionally a little bit too fast, forcing Mrs. Loveless to leap out of the way. She shouted something which was muffled by the car's engine, but whatever it was, it got the crowd's attention. Everybody turned their heads away from the station, towards Johnny's truck and the man handcuffed in the back seat.

"Gregory, we're gonna make a path through these people and you're gonna go straight inside, do you hear me?" Johnny called over his shoulder as he threw on the parking brake.

Gregory Rochester didn't respond.

"Seriously. Dude. This town is mad as a cat in a bathtub right now. They get a clear shot at you, somebody's gonna get hurt. So, when I open your door you put your head down and you make a beeline straight for that door which Sinclair is gonna unlock."

Johnny tossed the keys to Sinclair.

"Blue key. You go first. Get Cleese and O'Hare out here with some of the barricades from the basement. I want a path to that front door that's six feet wide at a minimum."

Sinclair nodded and opened his door. He hadn't expected the crowd's noise to be so loud. Everybody was screaming.

"Murderer."

"How could you?"

"It's Rochester! We knew it! We knew it was him! Just like his wife!"

Sinclair tuned it all out and muscled his way towards the door.

For the most part the towns folk let him by without issue. It wasn't him they were here to see.

Sinclair fumbled with Johnny's keychain, trying to force the red key into the lock, then switching to the blue key. Trying to turn the key to the left when it really needed to turn to the right.

A hand fell on Sinclair's shoulder just before he pushed the door inwards.

"Need a hand there, new buddy?"

Mayor Bellman's voice cut through the din of the crowd with unnatural ease. Typical politician. No matter how many people were ranting and screaming, somehow, they were always the ones finding a way to make their voices heard. It must have been some superpower all law schools taught to their sleazebags on day one.

Sinclair opened the door and tried to slip through on his own, but the Mayor made it through as well. Sinclair thought about protesting, forcing the man back into the street with the rest of the mob, but who knew how long that would take. He had to get the other officers to help get Johnny and Rochester in here. He didn't have time to wrestle a politician.

"I don't have time right now, sir. Sit over there. Stay out of our way."

"I can help. What do you need? Want that crowd to go away?"

"Just sit over there. Hey, Cleeese! O'Hare! Help me get those sawhorses up from the basement."

The Davis parents peeked out from Johnny's glass office, a bloody mass still seated silently between them. Shit. They couldn't see Rochester get dragged in here, could they?

Cleese showed up, materializing from somewhere near the back of the office.

"Sawhorses you said, Deputy?"

"Yeah. But no. You head up there and get the Davis family somewhere secure. The interrogation room or the evidence closet. I don't really care. Just nowhere with a window."

Cleese looked from Sinclair to Mayor Bellman, who nodded as if giving permission for Cleese to do what Sinclair was instructing.

The fucking nerve of that guy . . .

Sinclair would deal with it later, though. Too many issues now.

"Where's O'Hare?" Sinclair shouted at Cleese's back.

Cleese shrugged in response and Sinclair groaned. The sawhorses were too heavy to carry upstairs on his own.

Hating himself, Sinclair turned towards Mayor Bellman.

"Fine. You don't mind rolling your sleeves up? I could use a hand with some barricades. They're downstairs. Follow me."

The Mayor smiled, his dimples cutting victory lines into his cheeks. Now Sinclair would owe him one later. That's how all these politician-types thought. Lugging the sawhorses upstairs now was money in the bank, and Sinclair had taken the first step down the slippery slope of indebtitude.

But he couldn't think of that now.

With great effort, Sinclair and Mayor Bellman managed to move the heavy lumber bars upstairs and outside. Sinclair shouted for the townsfolk to move apart and got ignored. Mayor Bellman uttered a quick, indoor-volume command, and those close-by all fell away immediately.

Show-offy bastard.

But the barricades got set and Johnny opened the driver's side door of his truck, shot the Mayor a look that could have killed, and then pulled Rochester out of the back.

The crowd's shouting reached a new octave at the sight of the old man, slathered in his own healthy coat of blood, stepping down and walking between them. Some of the townsfolk threw things at him. Little plastic cups of room-temperature coffee. A spare coin from their purse. Nothing that could actually do damage, get an assault and battery charge levied their way, but enough to get their point across- they had decided Rochester was guilty. Before any evidence had been shown, and before even the crime had been defined, here walked the culprit.

With the Mayor's help, Johnny and Sinclair ushered their creepy ward into the safety of the station's interior.

"Well they certainly seem riled up today," the Mayor commented.

"What are you doing here?" Johnny turned on Bellman the moment the door was locked behind him.

"Well, I heard the rumors about what happened to dear Barker Davis and I wanted to lend a hand. It's my town after all. I've gotta make sure they feel safe."

"No, *we* need to make sure they feel safe. You need to get roads paved and shit like that. You don't need to be in the station right now, so get." Johnny snapped, all his frustration finally giving way.

Between the two men, Gregory Rochester chuckled, and the

sound was so unnatural it set the hairs on the back of Sinclair's neck on edge. His voice was more high pitched than Sinclair had expected, and the noise kept catching in the back of the man's throat as if he spoke through a wind-up music box that had been dropped one too many times.

"Help, he says?" the words whistled up from Rochester's throat. "Make them feel safe? Mayor, this is all your fault. All your fault. All your fault."

Rochester looked up, made eye contact with Johnny, then Sinclair, then finally the Mayor. "Your lies were crafted with strings attached. But you were too short sighted to see that, weren't you? You all were. This whole god damned town. You really thought you could get away with it, didn't you? Well, you can't just bury your secrets, Mr. Mayor." Rochester's lips curled up as he said the word Mayor.

"Not this time. None of you can. You think you can change the past by just ignoring it? By "moving on?" There is no moving on from this. Your sins have been given legs. Arms. Mouths and eyes. And now your sins are coming to get you."

Eyes crazy with excitement, Rochester waggled his fingers in the air like he was making a shadow puppet on the Mayor's face. Arms and legs waving about, coming for the Mayor's nose.

Johnny caught the lunatic's arm and pulled him away before he made contact.

"That's enough from you. Into holding until we decide what to do about the threat you just made to the Mayor. The damage you did to that little Davis kid."

"I didn't do anything to the Davis kid. He slipped and fell when he was trespassing in my house. Same as you. I never touched the munchkin."

"Sure. Whatever. Get into holding and we'll figure it out later.

Gregory did as he was told, walking into the secure room and taking a seat on the long metal bench which was bolted against the wall. The ancient toymaker looked at Johnny, looked at Sinclair, then averted his eyes down at his own hands, silently lost among his own thoughts again, the way he had been 99 percent of the time since he'd been picked up.

There was no fight to him. He didn't protest or argue. Just sat there in his cell, claiming innocence but accepting his situation with his sense of calm reclaimed.

“Get out, Mayor,” Johnny said again, but the insistence in his voice this time left no room for the politician to argue.

Bellman smiled his characteristic smile and nodded to the officers.

“Well looks like you’ve got things under control now,” he said, and his insinuation that they hadn’t been in control at any point irked Sinclair to his core. It was all he could do not to kick the man’s legs out from under him as he slipped back towards the door and the dispersing crowd outside.

“Glad to see you finally locked up where you belong, Rochester.” Bellman called just before the door closed, offering no chance for Johnny or Sinclair or Gregory to fire back a response of their own.

But in his cell, Gregory Rochester smiled. His arthritic fingers bent painfully at his knuckles as he danced with his hands in the air, making some invisible puppet bobble to and fro for his own imagined entertainment.

“Head back to that house, Sinclair,” Johnny ordered. “See what else you can turn up. We won’t be able to keep Rochester here for long without evidence. I can’t see the kook lawyering up, but still. Anything you can get will protect our asses. Yeah?”

Sinclair nodded, still watching the toymaker in his cell.

“Something’s wrong here,” Sinclair whispered.

“I know,” Johnny responded.

# RETURN TO DOLL HOUSE

**IT SEEMED LIKE** there were fewer dolls when Sinclair returned to the Rochester House.

He shut the engine of Johnny's truck off but left the keys in the ignition. The radiator clicked at him as it cooled slowly, and Sinclair scanned the windows of the house, the front yard, the porch, trying to pinpoint any one doll from earlier which had vanished. He wasn't just imagining this, was he? Maybe he was just expecting the dolls this time so their numbers appeared less striking.

But no. There were definitely fewer of them.

Right?

Maybe.

Sinclair needed a nap. Or just a full night of sleep, free from ghostly visits and strange dreams. Maybe just some damn coffee. But none of the above were on the schedule.

He pulled the keys free and swung the driver's door open, stepping onto Rochester's weed-riddled lawn for the second time that day. He stared at the dolls in the side yard which were arranged on a picnic blanket, a wicker basket between them with paper plates and plastic fruits passed out to each. Those fruits hadn't been there last time, had they?

Sinclair decided, officially, that he hated this place.

Trying to ignore the way the hairs were standing up on the back of his neck, and turning his back on the mannequins from the woods, which he could have sworn were looking at him, Sinclair soldiered forward into the house.

He pulled on a pair of plastic gloves which Johnny had slipped him- no contaminating the potential crime scene- and pushed the door open, moving inside before he could get any more creeped out.

Sinclair looked around, heart sinking in his chest. There were *definitely* less dolls inside.

But what did that mean? Did somebody else come by while the cops were at the station? Steal away . . . some . . . of the unsettling toys? For what purpose? Evidence tampering? Were the dolls somehow connected to all the blood that had coated Barker that morning?

Sinclair groaned and called into the house, trying to use his voice to scare away some of his own anxiety.

"Hollow Hills Sheriff's Department. Is anybody in here?"

Crickets in response.

Sinclair moved slowly, checking his corners as he moved, fingers hovering close to his right side, ready to grab his weapon or his phone if things took a sudden turn.

But as he moved, the house stayed quiet around him. Even the floorboards refrained from moaning or groaning, as if they were listening along with Rochester, trying to hear whatever he was trying to hear.

Clearing the first floor took no time at all. Rochester found a closet sparsely occupied by a pair of moth-eaten coats. The cupboard was mostly bare with just enough cans of spam and vienna sausages to keep a person alive for a few days. Maybe a week tops.

Then there was the door.

A trail of dark red, bloody footprints tracked away from the door; too small to have been Rochester's, Johnny's, or even Sinclair's.

Barker Davis, then.

Had to be.

So he was barking up the right tree after all. The story was coming together in Sinclair's mind, even if Barker had refused to tell it to him. The kid had snuck into the house for God knew what reason, gone to the basement, found something that coated him in blood, then he'd run back up the steps, dripping crimson, and racing through here.

Sinclair stood back up and scanned the rest of the kitchen, noticing more and more partial footprints from the basement door and the back door leading outside. No heels were present in any of the bloodstains. Just toes. All of the kids' weight had been forward. He'd been running. Getting the hell out of this house just as fast as he could.

Another bloody print caught Sinclair's attention, giving him pause until he recognized the shape of a peacock's foot.

"The bloody bird was here too? What the fuck, kid."

Sinclair couldn't help but roll his eyes. He looked at the dolls on the couch for some sort of validation that all this was ridiculous, but the toys just stared back at him, their permanently painted smiles just adding to the absurdity.

Why had Sinclair moved here again?

He returned to the kitchen, found the basement door again with the biggest, most pronounced bloody footprint at its base, and took a deep breath, to try to recenter himself.

Sinclair gripped the doors handle and found it frigid to the touch despite the warmth of the day. He took a deep breath, swung the door open, and was hit in the face by a rush of air escaping the low pressure of the basement.

The far side of the door greeted him, dark and damp, and the smell of stale blood washed up from that darkness, smothering Sinclair and causing him to pull his shirt collar up over his nose.

Whatever was down there causing this smell, Sinclair had clearly found the evidence Johnny was looking for.

Sinclair reached inside carefully and found the light switch. He flicked it uselessly once, twice, three and four times before giving up and pulling his phone from his pocket, turning his flashlight on, and groaning.

He didn't want to go down there.

Whatever Rochester was up to, whatever created this heavy bloody smell, it wasn't going to be good.

Damn this job.

Sinclair stepped down the old wooden steps carefully, one at a time, nudging the debris from Johnny's earlier fall out of his way before settling his whole weight on any of the creaking boards.

It felt like he descended forever. No basement could be this far underground. Was this actually some bomb shelter from the Cold War era? Had the whole basement collapsed down into a sinkhole, the stairs somehow extending along with the wreckage?

Sinclair toed the next step, settled on it. Toed the next step. Settled on it.

The heavy, damp aura of the basement felt like it was swallowing Sinclair. Consuming him and dragging him down to join in what was surely just a pool of blood flooding the basement, if the stench was any indication.

His shoe landed on something hard and unforgiving, lacking the sag that the steps had given. The new surface was scratchy and sticky. Oh, so sticky. The basement floor. Concrete, most likely. He crouched, just off the bottom step, and investigated the floor. A pile of laundry was to his left. Shirts, pants, and little plastic slippers had been discarded in a heap, and they stank to high heaven.

Sinclair swung his phone around again, the light from the doorway overhead failing to support him in the slightest anymore, the beam of his flashlight disappearing into his inky-black surroundings uselessly, finding nothing to land on or illuminate except more and more empty space.

The basement must have been an absolute cavern. How could he see nothing? How had Barker made it all the way down here on his own? All the way back up? What had he found, down here in the darkness? HAD he seen anything, or had he just anticipated the source of the bloody smell and turned tail before his eyes adjusted? Maybe that's why Barker wasn't giving him or Johnny any answers. Maybe he just didn't know what the hell he had stumbled into.

Something came at Sinclair out of the dark, his flashlight catching the red glint of flayed muscles and congealed blood just a split second before Sinclair walked face-first into it.

The blood slapping his face was cold, with any of its body heat long ago drained away, and the weight of the skinned body knocked Sinclair backwards, almost tackling him to the ground, but Sinclair spun around in his shock, and slicked his cheek along the bloody mass, managing to just barely salvage his balance in the darkness.

Whatever he had just bumped into rushed away from him, hiding back in the darkness from whence it came, but then returning as a red blur, rushing towards him with even more speed.

Sinclair dodged, weaving to his right as the object swung through the space he had just occupied. He tracked the movement with his phone, illuminating two legs suspended in the air, bound by a rope. A long torso. Arms. An oblong head.

It wasn't human.

The mass of skinless muscle that was down here was a beast.

It swung back again, a red blur in the darkness, moving slower this time. Sinclair stepped out of its way with a bit less panic in his step, his phone's light finding the taught rope above the animal. He calmed himself down enough to actually identify it. The thing was a flayed sheep, suspended on a hook from the ceiling above as if Sinclair was in a meat packing plant. Or maybe it was a goat. It was hard to tell with it moving around so much. Not that Sinclair could have identified a flayed sheep from a flayed goat even when it was sitting still, but the rest of the tension released from Sinclair's shoulders as the nightmarish conjurings of his imagination were replaced by reality.

This dead animal, whatever type of animal it was, had been hung down here, suspended from the ceiling, and Sinclair had bumped it, explaining the movement. Nothing was attacking him.

Sinclair almost had to smile at the absurdity of it. Almost.

Instead, he stepped around the dead animal as it slowed, then stopped its swinging.

The smell made more sense now. Rochester had been slaughtering game in his basement. Bleeding it out. Of course the air was heavy with the scent of iron and copper.

He aimed his light at the floor and looked around until he found the drain in what was *probably* the center of the room and he tried to orient himself with it as his point of reference. Just beside the drain lay an enormous bird, and Sinclair's first thought was that it was a turkey. Then he saw the way his light caught the bird's tail feathers. The plume atop its head. Peacock. Was this what Barker had been doing down here? Chasing after his bird? It was dead, blood pooled around its throat which had evidently been slit.

This was all making more and more sense. Of course a butcher's shop in the basement of a house in the middle of the woods was ridiculous, but as far as rational explanations for all the blood on Barker Davis, this was probably as logical and, thankfully, as innocent, as Sinclair could have hoped for. Why Rochester would have decided to butcher the boy's bird was still up in the air. Maybe they could bring a destruction of property charge against him? But if the bird had come into Rochester's house, then he could claim . . . what? Self-defense? Were peacocks dangerous enough to justify that?

Legal questions ping-ponging around in his head, Sinclair spun his light about, observing the rest of the bodies hanging, suspended all around him. He approached them one at a time, careful not to crash into them the way he had run into the first one. They were all the same. Fat, thick thighs. Short, stumpy legs. A long middle leading to the animal's head. No horns, Sinclair confirmed. So, sheep, not goats, assuming Sinclair's memories from his 9th grade animal science classes could be trusted.

Maybe, more specifically, they were lambs?

Did Rochester have a small farm around here? When had he made the transition from toy making to butchering? Was there some natural progression from carving wooden puppets to carving flanks of steak? Maybe a blade was a blade and a substance was a substance?

It was weird as shit. But probably not illegal.

Sinclair kept panning around the room as he thought, his feet sticking to the floor in the places where the blood had coagulated the most. It took him a while in the dark, but he gradually managed to clear the entire basement, passing more and more and more dead animals until finally, in the farthest recess of the room, Sinclair discovered the work bench.

It was nestled in the deepest corner of the basement, surrounded by bloody tools and a trio of puppets which had been arranged with their backs propped against the concrete back wall. A little stool sat before the bench, and the puppets stared forward towards where the lambs had been slaughtered as if they had watched the whole procedure. Sinclair tried not to look too closely at the creepy dolls, instead aiming his attention towards the thing which sat in the middle of the bench.

Set neatly in the center of the workbench, with the surrounding blood stains and tools all giving it a wide berth, lay a small, leatherbound book. It looked like a journal, its pages yellowed and stiff, its binding cracked and old. Sinclair reached out a hand and picked the book up with a strange sort of reverence. All at once he felt like the book might disintegrate at his touch, collapsing with the weight of its age, but also that it might lash out at him, unleashing some devastating force that ripped the breath from his lungs.

Sinclair was so distracted by the feeling of the leather between his fingers that he failed to see his wife until she was nearly on top of him.

"Fuck!" he screamed and he stumbled backwards, the work bench hitting his hip, spinning him around, and sending his phone and its light skittering away towards the butchered lambs. The book stayed in his hands somehow, despite his fingers flying open, despite his hand definitely, maybe, letting go of it as he fell.

Sinclair had never seen his wife's ghost so close before, not in broad daylight, and the horror of her scorched and half-melted face broke him in an instant. The sight of her skin cracked around the black, charred flesh, coupled with the sudden smell of burning hair sent him stumbling to the ground. He was crying, tears flooding his eyes immediately, graciously obscuring his view of Claire's wounds. He leaned, hard, against the bench behind him, begging the wood for some stability.

"You're not really here," he whispered to his wife.

But she didn't seem to agree.

The ghostly figure moved closer to Sinclair and maybe it was just the smell of the lambs corrupting his senses, but Sinclair imagined he could smell her burnt flesh. It triggered his memories of the accident, teleporting him back to that day when his world had ended.

Sinclair kicked at the ground, trying to slide himself away from the wife that he so desperately wanted to embrace one more time. But he could not. Not like this. Not when her reemergence was so obviously a lie, a trick of his morbid imagination.

He needed to get out.

He turned away from Claire just as she was about to make contact with him, shoving his way through one of the lambs. The livestock swung around on its hook and battered Sinclair's face with a smear of its sticky, cool blood. Sinclair ignored it though. Bent down as quickly as possible to scoop up his phone, and then bounded for the steps.

Behind him, the ghastly figure of his wife might have pursued. Or maybe she stayed at that work bench, staring after him, her empty dead eyes tracking his path through the darkness. He would never know. He refused to look back.

This was wrong.

So wrong.

The house was playing tricks on him, surely. The sight of the bloody kid, his fear of the dark, it was just all too much for Sinclair to process in such a small window. He needed to go home. Needed to sleep. Then he would realize that all this had been just a strange, overblown nightmare. There was no way his wife had followed him here. No way that her ghost had come after him in broad daylight like that.

But the book in his hands was real. The book that Sinclair couldn't, or wouldn't, put down despite his understanding that he was taking evidence from a crime scene. He should have photographed the entire location, documented where the book was, called in a forensics squad to turn the place over, made sure that every drop of blood in that hell hole was really goats blood or lambs blood or sheep's blood or what-the-fuck-ever.

But he didn't.

Instead, he just clutched the book against his chest for reasons unfathomable, and he ran. He didn't slow down as he reached the Rochester House's front door. He threw it open with his shoulder and fell, stumbling into the cool, pleasant light of a North Georgia late evening. Around him, crickets ceased their usual song, shocked into silence by Sinclair's unexpected outburst.

The mannequins in the woods watched as Sinclair vomited up his lunch, his forehead sweating in tracks around the lamb's congealed blood, his knees weak.

"Fuck this place," he grumbled, spit dribbling past his lips.

He knew he hadn't secured the whole house. There were at least two rooms upstairs that he'd never set foot in. But it didn't matter. Not anymore. What he had seen in the basement was probably enough to piece the whole story together. The book in his hands was bound to have answers. It was probably just some butcher's manual, or a journal of goat raising instructions. Some ridiculous agrarian shit like that. He would go back, fill Johnny in, and then they would probably release Rochester the next morning once he gave them the full story about how he was just raising his own livestock and meat packing in his basement as some perverted, weird little hobby. Like peacock farming. Or doll making. Or some shit like that. These Hollow Hills folks and their hobbies . . .

Sinclair listened to see if he could hear any other, still alive sheep baa-ing somewhere deeper in the Rochester's property. But heard and saw nothing save for the silent stares of the two mannequins and the curious dolls, most of their heads turned, staring towards the road through the woods. Staring towards Sinclair.

Had they been like that when he first arrived?

It didn't matter. He was leaving.

Sinclair climbed into Johnny's truck and backed down the gravel drive again, making a point of not looking back at the house. He didn't want to see his wife in the window, in the doorway, sitting around with the dolls on the plaid blanket, bringing a make-believe sandwich up to the still-intact half of her mouth and pretending to chew.

He just wanted to get away.

# HI-YO SILVER

SINCLAIR DIDN'T TELL Johnny anything about what happened at the house. Not immediately. Instead, he drove to his house, parked Johnny's truck in his driveway, and went inside to shower. He needed a minute to calm down and clear his head. The Station was all the way on the other side of town.

Sinclair stripped off his uniform and threw the blood-soaked garments straight into the trash. No amount of Tide would have saved them. He'd have to report that once he got to the station and grabbed another uniform from the closet in the locker room.

It took almost fifteen minutes in the shower to get all of the blood off himself. The drain water ran bright red, then pink, then pink, then still pink nearly forever as if the lamb's blood had seeped into Sinclair's skin and was just slowly leeching out bit by bit.

But it was fine.

Sinclair needed the time to process his thoughts with his eyes closed, his skin warmed by the gently massage which the pressurized shower head provided.

His wife had been in that house. She wasn't some figment of his imagination or some night terror that he couldn't shake, the way he had assumed she was at night, in bed.

He had seen her.

He had smelled her.

Damnit, he had nearly touched her.

What this meant, he didn't know yet. But it gave his beaten, deflated heart something that resembled a pulse for the first time in months. Hope was a hell of a drug. Hope in what? Sinclair didn't know, and it didn't matter. He had found hope nonetheless.

He finished up in the shower and toweled off. Climbed free from the glass and porcelain cage to find Rochester's book sitting beside his bathroom sink. He didn't remember bringing the book inside. Didn't remember clearing off a spot for it between his toothbrush and deodorant. But he didn't remember much about coming home in general. Fugue state would be putting it too dramatically, but Sinclair definitely hadn't been thinking straight.

He approached the book and lifted its cover, flipping through the pages and glancing at the contents.

The pages were yellowed and browned, illustrated with a mess of diagrams, star charts, images of demons, pentagrams, and witches all hastily scribbled in something like charcoal. It all reminded Sinclair of the Necronomicon from those bad horror movies.

"You're shitting meeeeee." Sinclair complained as he turned the pages, still wrapped in nothing more than a towel.

Among the images, some script had been written in two different hands. One light, flowy cursive in a language that Sinclair didn't recognize. Written in something less prominent than ink and slightly red tinged. More blood. Of course it was. The second script was in English. Clunky, blocky letters, etched by a pencil in the margins around everything else, as if this was some textbook that a college student had been marking up while preparing for a test.

"Blood required, but human blood? Could animal blood work?" The questions had been scribbled next to an image of a human having their throat cut, their life dribbling down the page towards a second body with its eyes closed, down below the ground.

Sinclair turned the page.

"Resurrection" was written in pencil. A word so terrifying and ridiculous and hopeful that Sinclair's breath caught in his throat.

He didn't believe in magic. He thought that all tales of the paranormal or the religious were just false promises meant to keep fools occupied. Cheap ways to peddle reality TV to the masses. Children's performers making quick cash at birthday parties.

But after seeing Claire at the Rochester House and experiencing everything in that basement firsthand, suddenly Sinclair found that the word hit differently. The word didn't seem quite as ridiculous as it should have. Sinclair's fingers trembled and he sat down on his bathroom stool, turning to the next page carefully.

Huge black X's covered the next page, and the next, and the next, growing more and more pronounced and heavy as somebody's frustration -Rochster's?- boiled over into the book.

Eight pages later, an un-X'd page showed a voodoo doll, pins shoved through its button eyes. Here, the sketches stopped, giving way instead to nine pages filled exclusively by flowy, foreign cursive. Sinclair scanned over notes upon notes of the illegible instructions and warnings, with questions and comments squeezed into the margins by the second, pencil-wielding commenter.

Sinclair lost himself in those pages, looking for any sort of promise that this could be real.

Time lost its meaning until there came a boom and a crash from downstairs.

Sinclair slapped the book closed and slipped it into the drawer of his bathroom sink as Johnny shouted from the front door.

"You son of a bitch, you were supposed to bring my truck back!"

Oops.

"And what are these boxes *still* doing here? Jesus, man. Unpack already. What are you waiting for? An HGTV special? Packrats R Us?"

There was a crash from downstairs as Johnny fell over or under or through something and Sinclair hurried to the top of the stairs.

"And why don't you . . . SHIT MAN, PUT SOME CLOTHES ON!"

Sinclair looked down and realized he was still in his towel. However much time had passed in the bathroom, his hair was dry now and the towel swished around his bare thighs like an embroidered kilt of some sort.

He stood still, not quite sure what to do, as his boss stood at the bottom of the stairs with an unfortunate view.

"Put your damn clothes on!" Johnny shouted a second time, and now Sinclair was spurred into action.

Behind him, Sinclair heard Johnny uttering curses under his breath and calling Sinclair all sorts of names. He threw the flaps back on a tall box which was labeled 'summer clothes' and quickly slipped into briefs, shorts, and a T-shirt, assuming he didn't need to put another uniform on for the day. By the time he returned downstairs, Johnny was sitting on his plastic-wrapped couch, head in his hands.

"You decent this time, deputy?"

"Uh-huh."

"Well good." Johnny lifted his head up. "You know this place would feel a hell of a lot more like a home if you unpacked literally anything, right? Stacks of beige cardboard don't quite sell the 'Welcome Home' concept."

Sinclair nodded but didn't really answer as he settled onto the couch next to Johnny.

"Sorry about the truck. I lost track of time. That house . . . "

"Yeah. Status report. What did we find?"

"There are dead animals in the basement."

Johnny's eyes nearly popped out of his head.

"Like, goats or sheep or something like that. Like his basement is a butcher shop. Not like a bunch of dead kittens or anything weird."

"Butcher shop in your basement is pretty freaking weird."

"Yeah, but like . . . not malicious maybe. Right? We're in the middle of nowhere. Raising your own livestock is a rural thing, isn't it?"

"I guess it could be. It's not common, but it's also not as absurd as it would have been in Charlotte." Johnny said this a bit under his breath as he tapped his knee with a finger, frowning and looking around the room.

"So maybe Rochester is innocent of any crime? Is there a chance Barker just stumbled into a blood-letting or something, and his innocent little mind made a mountain out of a mole hill."

"Barker Davis doesn't have anything resembling an innocent mind."

"You know what I mean."

"Yeah, I do. And maybe. But I don't want to let Rochester go just yet. Seems like there's more to this than we've uncovered so far. No signs of living animals anywhere around the house, right? No goat pens or anything like that?"

"I thought of that too, and no. Nothing like that."

"Then yeah. Something's still up. Livestock doesn't just pop up out of the weeds like that. Rochester must have gone through a lot of trouble to get his hands on goats without anybody in town noticing a goat truck driving through. Or to keep goats raised, himself, without anybody hearing or smelling them. You're sure they were goats?"

"I mean. Sort of? That or sheep. Would there be a difference?"

"Not that I know . . . "

The two of them sat in silence, mulling the mystery over as the fan creaked overhead.

After a few minutes, Johnny leaned forward, pressed against his knees to help him rise, and said "Go get my damn keys and meet me outside. I brought a surprise for you."

Sinclair did as he was told, returning upstairs to the bathroom where Johnny's truck keys had been discarded and giving the drawer with the book a wide berth. When he got outside, he found Johnny standing beside an old, rusty six-speed bike.

"Thanks, dad. This is the best sixth birthday ever," Sinclair joked, and Johnny laughed.

Sinclair tossed the keys to Johnny's truck to him.

"I'm not driving all the way across town twice a day anymore to get your bum ass to work. So, the way I see it, you've got two options here, champ. Either you fix up your car there, get that flat taken care of, and start driving yourself around town like an adult . . . "

" . . . or . . . "

"Jesus, Sinclair. Just fix your damn car. What's the big hangup? Or you go inside, get some dusty-ass Tom Glavine baseball card from one of those boxes, shove it in the spokes, and make sure it makes a decent sound before you go pedaling your way to work."

Sinclair glanced at his car and saw Max's car seat in the back. He couldn't get back in there. It had nearly killed him driving to Hollow Hills in the memory box, his eyes blurring with tears as he navigated 80 miles per hour on the highway. He'd found the rumble strips more than once.

Sinclair stepped forward to investigate the bike.

"You serious? I thought I was getting this for you as a joke," Johnny laughed, but the joke didn't quite reach his eyes. There was concern there. Genuine, warranted, concern, Sinclair knew. But he wasn't able to face his past. Not yet. He still needed more time to heal. And if that meant riding a bike to work for a few days, weeks, months, or years, then that was just the price he'd have to pay.

"So, what are our next steps with Rochester?" Sinclair tried to change the subject.

Johnny scoffed and rolled the bike over to Sinclair.

"Dunno. If what you said is true, and there's nothing else in that house, then we don't have much to hold him on. I'll look up the laws about domestic slaughter of animals. Maybe there's something actually illegal about that. Who the hell knows. But when it turns out that you can do whatever you want to livestock on your own property, which I suspect is the case, then we'll have to let him go in the morning. Guy gives me the damn creeps, but that's no reason to keep him booked."

Sinclair nodded and opened his mouth. He should have told Johnny about the book. He should have told him there were still two rooms upstairs that he hadn't checked out.

He closed his mouth instead.

Johnny climbed into his truck and revved the engine.

"You didn't even top off the tank?"

Sinclair sat on the bike's seat, tested the pedals, and found the whole device to be about the right size for him actually.

"You better be careful, newbie. A few more instances like this and the Sheriff'll fire your ass."

Sinclair forced a smile for his old friend, knowing his words were a joke, but thinking he heard a hint of seriousness backing the words as well. Johnny was great. But his patience would only stretch so far. He was only human.

"Enjoy your day off tomorrow. Get some work done around here and try to get your head right, bud. Remember: Even when you get a new start in this life, its still up to you to get off the start line yourself. I'll see you at the station on Sunday!"

With that, Johnny left the house, backing out of the driveway and leaving Sinclair tooling around on the bike, surrounded by weeds, his busted-up car, and his busted-up thoughts.

# SILENT NIGHT, DEADLY NIGHT

**THAT NIGHT,** as Sinclair wrestled with his usual nightmares and Johnny lay passed out on his desk at the station, computer screen glowing with information about state approved sheep slaughtering protocols, Mayor Bellman tipped back the last of an expensive glass of bourbon.

It was late. Later than Bellman usually stayed up, but tonight he was celebrating.

Gregory Rochester was finally in jail.

Not that he'd really proved to be much of a nuisance to Bellman these past few years, but just the fact that Rochester was out there in the world, knowing what he knew, suspecting what he suspected, it had put Bellman in a position of weakness. There had been a constant threat of Rochester snapping and running his mouth to the wrong people, ruining everything Bellman and the Gattises had built here in Hollow Hills. More than once, Bellman had toyed with plans to silence the man himself, but they were all too risky. Too uncertain for him to ever willingly act on. Especially after last time.

But it had all worked out, hadn't it? The old loon had painted *himself* into a corner and now all Bellman had to do was find the right lawyer, some cutthroat shark of a litigator, and he could have Rochester gone for good. No more loose ends.

He set his glass down on his nightstand and felt a sense of calm which had eluded him for years. He climbed into bed, his wife already fast asleep and lightly snoring beside him. Tomorrow he would reach out to Hal Sharpton. Hal was a true-blue bastard. A mean son of a bitch who attacked the courtroom like a rabid dog whenever he got the scent of something good. Something with money. He would be perfect. Then Bellman's road to reelection would be paved for him, not that he'd anticipated any real competition to start with. Arresting and removing the town's freakshow would have the public singing his praises, especially after everybody saw him at the station today assisting in the arrest. He was a mayor who was willing to roll up his sleeves, get his hands dirty, they'd all say.

Some of them would even know how true that statement really was.

The gears in his head spinning, his delusions of grandeur amplified by his slight inebriation, Bellman found it hard to fall asleep immediately.

Which was part of how he found himself awake, still, at about 2:30 when his front window shattered. From all the way upstairs, the noise came across as little more than a slight tinkling sound, but it was enough to catch the Mayor's attention and rose from bed in the middle of the night.

Bellman grabbed a baseball bat from out of his closet and reopened the bedroom door.

All seemed quiet on the upstairs landing. Both of his kids' doors were closed and the Mayor heard nothing but his kids white noise machines hissing from within their rooms. There was no pitter-patter of his children's tiny feet downstairs which might have explained a knocked over lamp or a dropped glass or otherwise. Nope. All seemed silent.

Bellman retreated into his room, found his slippers, then made his way to the closer of the two circular staircases which led to the main floor. He kept a tight grip on the handle of his bat and stared down towards the first floor, tiptoeing as quietly as he could manage, the bat cocked and ready over his shoulder.

The front entryway was littered with broken glass that reflected light from the kitchen. Mrs. Bellman insisted on keeping the light from their oven hood perpetually burning through the night, in case one of the kids woke up and started wandering the house before the sun.

Bellman made it to the main landing and looked around to his left and right.

The slim window to the left of the front door had been blown inwards. That much was apparent. But what had blown out the glass, Bellman couldn't tell. The Mayor wandered back and forth looking for signs of anything that might have caused the damage. No brick or ball or rock lay in the front lobby, though.

Doing his best detective impression, Bellman tried to think through what else might have happened.

Maybe a fist, then? Maybe some robber knocked the glass out so they could reach an arm in, unfasten the lock from the back side?

Bellman investigated the door and found the latch still fastened. But that didn't really prove anything, did it? A burglar could have easily let themselves inside, then latched the door behind them, making it *seem* like they'd never come in.

So maybe it was a stealthy robber, then? One who was trying to cover their tracks?

The night was getting interesting.

"Mayor Bellman protects own home from intruder."

The headline would play especially well with male voters aged 20-40. He wondered what would make the front page of the Hollow Gazette. His heroism or Rochester's demise?

He turned around slowly, dragging his slippers instead of stepping so that he could avoid crunching any of the glass on the ground; making as little noise as possible as he crept towards the kitchen. He checked his corners as he snuck, trying to make sure no robber could get the jump on him.

The kitchen was empty.

The dishwasher hummed softly from when their housekeeper had filled it after dinner and set it to run. The pantry sat, closed, apparently undisturbed.

Not a fool, Bellman grabbed the handle to the pantry, whipped it open with his bat held at the ready.

Empty.

Cans of vegetables, baskets full of bread, and various cheeses stared innocently back at him until Bellman closed the door slowly, quietly.

He turned and made his way through the saloon-doors which separated the kitchen from the dining area and peered through the slats at the darkness beyond.

The dining room was just as vacant as the kitchen had been.

"Where is this fucker?" Bellman whispered to himself, his excitement at hunting an intruder quickly giving way to frustration.

The main floor's bathroom was empty, as was the laundry room, as was the coat closet. Bellman stabbed the coats in the closet with his baseball bat, hoping to hear a yelp, but there was nothing. The silence of the house around him seemed to be taunting him at this point.

Maybe there wasn't an intruder after all. Maybe the window had just shattered.

It was stupid, but the illogical thought kept bouncing around Bellman's head, causing his irritation to deepen.

Maybe the window had been fractured long before and the pressure from the cold house coupled with the heat outside had just maybe broken it the rest of the way . . . maybe?

He walked into the living room carelessly, having mostly given up on finding anything of note.

The doll was seated in the middle of the coffee table, and the appearance of it, with its striking blue eyes reflecting some undiscernable light source, caused Bellman to yelp and almost drop his bat.

It was an old ventriloquist's dummy. Its jaw hung slack, but otherwise the puppet sat straight up with perfect posture. Brown plastic had been molded on its head to imitate slicked back brown hair and its suit bore a striking similarity to one of the suits Bellman threw on whenever he was on the campaign trail.

The damn maid. She was supposed to clean up all of the kids' toys before she left. Emphasis on "all" of the toys.

The mayor checked under the couches and behind his easy chair, making sure the doll wasn't just some distraction the intruder was using to sneak up on him.

But no.

Bellman was still alone.

The Mayor groaned and tapped his bat against his foot.

He lifted the doll up by the throat and carried it with him as he checked the other rooms, humbly performing the maid's job for her. He would bring the doll upstairs to Emma's room. It was more likely hers than Keith's. He liked video games nowadays. Dolls and action figures were more Emma's thing, he was pretty sure.

Bellman would dock the maid's pay tomorrow to teach her a lesson about thoroughness.

The doll felt warm in his hands like maybe some electronics inside were malfunctioning, and its eyes did that trick where they seemed like they were always following you.

Bellman hated it.

He cleared the rest of the house quickly, hurrying so that he could go back upstairs to drop the doll near his kids' door and be done with it. The effects of the whiskey were wearing off, and the adrenaline that accompanied a possible home invasion had dulled. Exhaustion from a long day finally caught up to him and by the time Bellman had checked around their home gym he didn't much care if there really was an intruder anymore.

Maybe the window had just shattered on its own.

Maybe some small pebble from outside had been slung about on the wind and broken through, lying now among the shards of glass.

He'd find it first thing in the morning, for sure. How silly of him to assume somebody was in his house. Right? Stray pebbles shattering a window was totally normal. Probably. Maybe.

His slippers slapped the wooden staircase as Bellman ascended, wavering slightly in his drunken, sleep-deprived disorientation.

Emma's room was closed, so the Mayor laid what he thought was his daughter's doll against the door, propping it up so it would fall inwards when Emma awoke. He looked at the doll again as he backed away, its eyes still catching whatever blue light it had reflected downstairs. He scanned the upstairs landing, trying for a second time to determine the source of the glow. There was a yellow nightlight glowing down the hall, but nothing blue.

Oh well.

The Mayor backed away from the toy, blaming his delusions and weird conclusions on the late hour, the good whiskey, and just the whole Rochester situation from earlier. He hadn't thought the loon had gotten into his head, but he was certainly feeling jumpier than usual tonight.

Bellman passed through his bedroom, his wife still snoring on her half of the bed, and entered the bathroom. He relieved himself, kicked off his slippers, and returned the room, ready to pass out.

Maybe if he had been sober, Bellman would have noticed the way his wife had suddenly stopped snoring.

Maybe if it hadn't been three in the morning, Bellman would have realized that somebody, or something, had closed the bedroom door behind him.

Maybe if Bellman hadn't still been daydreaming about news articles about himself, he would have noticed the wires which had been draped across his covers, the glitter of fishing hooks tied to their ends.

Maybe. Maybe. Maybe.

Bellman climbed into bed, laying right on top of a series of thin metal that zig-zagged like mesh over the comforter. He tugged on the blanket, confused why it wouldn't budge.

From the darkness, something jerked ends of the strings and the hooks sprang to life, lurching towards Bellman, piercing his skin, and shoving their jagged tips deep through muscle and tissue until they raked at his bones. One hook caught the side of the Mayors neck, burying itself deep in the crook between his shoulder blade and his collar bone. Another caught him behind his knee cap as another ripped a gash in his scrotum. At least twenty others found purchase all up and down his body, simultaneously ravishing their pounds of flesh.

Bellman screamed as he felt his body pierced like a pincushion.

It was a wonder that such a wild, desperate sound didn't wake his children, even with their white noise machines set at full blast.

He tried to resist the onslaught, but the hooks tore at his skin from every angle. No matter which direction he pulled, his struggles drew the wires more and more taught.

His hot blood coated the sheets and soaked into the mattress as Bellman thrashed back and forth, screaming at the top of his lungs, hoping Mrs. Bellman might hear him. But the bed was empty beside him, with Mrs. Bellman already pulled into the darkness.

From the shadows, little arms pulled on their ends of the lines, setting their hooks deeper and deeper into their prey until finally, with a sudden, coordinated heave, the hooks all heaved in the same direction at once to rip Bellman free from his bed.

His head cracked against the floor as he landed, and Bellman was silenced by the blow.

In the absence of his cries, the Mayor's house returned to its typical, middle-of-the-night, regularly scheduled orchestra of soothing sounds. The kids' sound machines whirred away, the wind caused an American flag to flap about on the front porch, and if not for the scraping sounds of a body being dragged down the concrete driveway, things might have seemed entirely natural around Mayor Bellman's residence.

# HANG YOUR SECRETS HANG THEM UP HANG THEM UP NOW

**SINCLAIR WOKE UP** the next morning wracked with guilt. He should have told Johnny about the damn book. But he had gotten selfish and greedy when he saw that word. *Resurrection.* Gods, the promises that word held. In response he had abandoned his duties to the Sheriff's Department, to the town.

He had to go back today. He had to tell Johnny about *everything* he had found in the house, no matter how ridiculous it may seem, and no matter the potential charges for evidence tampering that could be filed. Johnny wouldn't do that to him.

It was supposed to be Sinclair's day off. Johnny, Cleese, and O'Hare should have handled the paperwork of releasing Gregory Rochester back into the wilds and Sinclair would or should have had a day to finally unpack a couple of his boxes.

But that just wouldn't sit right with him.

He couldn't just tool around the house, knowing that there was still a chance -infinitesimal as it might be- that Rochester was actually guilty of something. What, he didn't know, but a book of black magic sure seemed like an omen of misdoings. He couldn't let the man get released until he knew for sure.

And he couldn't just call Johnny, tell him that he hadn't done his job. Johnny would have understood, probably, but the pitying way he would baby Sinclair moving forward was too steep of a consequence. Johnny already thought Sinclair's mental state was fragile. What happened when he told him that he was seeing ghosts? Stealing books on the off chance that they contained magic spells to bring back his wife and dead son?

Sinclair made his way downstairs, unpacked his coffee pot, and tested out the pedals and the wheels on his new bike. The chain was old and the tires were nearly bald, but the thing would probably ride well enough.

Johnny had bought it for Sinclair as a joke, he was sure. Some smart-ass, passive aggressive nudge to get Sinclair to get his car back in working order. But it wasn't as simple as that. Climbing back in that car would mean having to look at the car seat in the back. It would mean smelling the vanilla air freshener that Claire insisted he hang from the rear view mirror. It would mean locking himself in a box with the ghosts for however long it took him to get to the station that day; a ten minute drive assuming he didn't pull over to the side of the road to bawl his eyes out, which he would.

No, his car was going to stay in the driveway a little while longer. The flat tire would stay flat and the ghosts would have to wait. Sinclair glanced up, towards where his bathroom was located with the blood-journal of black magic stowed away in a drawer. He wanted to go back upstairs. Wanted to flip through the book again. But based on the way he lost time yesterday, that wasn't a good idea. Whether it was some sort of a curse or just his own failure to monitor time, he couldn't afford to lose another day to its pages.

Sinclair cringed as he sipped his coffee, clamped the thermos' lid tightly shut, then wheeled the bicycle towards Main Street. He would do his due diligence at the Rochester House by checking behind those last few doors upstairs to convince himself that nothing else was amiss. Then he would come back, collect the book, and bring it to Johnny the way he was supposed to.

The fresh air and the gentle exercise of pedaling the bike helped clear Sinclair's mind a bit. He felt childish, but not necessarily in a bad way, as he forced the wheels into motion beneath him and flew down Hazel street. The ride gave him time to think, helped clear his head. A day was a long time. He could do more than just follow through on the house. After Sinclair checked the Rochester residence and cleared his conscience, maybe Sinclair could return home to get *at least* the kitchen of his new house in working order. Would that feel . . . good? Would that help him to feel unstuck in life?

Cooking food was good therapy. He knew that in theory. Remembered it from the days when Claire and Max were alive. Cooking was just involved enough that you didn't get distracted with other thoughts, but also just mindless enough to be calming.

And, if Sinclair was being honest about it, he considered himself to be a pretty decent cook. He could at least make something that tasted better than the grease traps Johnny had been dragging him to since he arrived. Mama Jeans was delicious, but he was sure it had taken a year off his life already.

If he could do all that: get the house cleared, get the kitchen established, and get some good food into himself, then maybe he could feel . . . dare he hope . . . positive? Encouraged? Just making his own way to work this morning was empowering, shifting his mindset. There was no telling what a whole day of task accomplishments could do for him.

Sinclair slammed on the brakes.

His eyes rose up, towards the branches of the maples which hung over Main Street's approach to town, towards the grotesque horrors which those branches now held, suspended over the road.

"What the actual fuck?"

The mayor swayed gently above Sinclair, blood dripping from his bare feet, plopping to the asphalt just in front of Sinclair's front tire.

Mayor Bellman had been stripped naked, the exposure probably meant to showcase his mutilation, but instead so much blood caked his arms and his torso that it was hard to make out where the wounds began and ended. His tendons and the ligaments had been popped and pulled clean from his frame, stretching high above the dead man to pull his arms and legs up at odd angles, the far ends tied to branches overhead. The dead man hung by a combination of his innards, metal wires, and neon fishing line, suspended in a pose like a puppet over a stage.

Bellman rocked back and forth gently on the cool, early-morning breeze, his tie soaked crimson and stuck to the gaping wound in his chest. When that same wind pushed the branches overhead about, it caused the bleeding man-puppet's arms to dance about slightly, his legs to bounce awkwardly, causing it to look like maybe Bellman might still be alive, might still be struggling to get down.

But no.

A river of blood had collected on the street, completely obscuring the double yellow lines that had been painted there. There was no way the man was still alive.

Sinclair stifled a scream as his plans for the day, like everything else in his life, fell into ruin. His legs pistoned the pedals of his bike in little circles and Sinclair raced past where the Mayor hung, feeling some of Bellman's blood drip onto his head.

Sinclair made it to the station, setting new land speed records for bike riding and threw open the doors.

"Johnny! Crime scene on Main Street. It's the mayor. We have to go get him down before anybody from town sees that he's dead as fuck and—" Sinclair paused, gasping for breath, trying to understand what he was seeing.

The other three members of the Sheriff's Department were all crowded around the station's holding cell, staring inside at Gregory Rochester.

It was like deja vu.

Gregory Rochester was covered in blood, standing on the metal bench which was bolted against the cell's back wall. His arms were held above his head, assuming the exact same pose the Mayor had been suspended in. His elbows and limp wrists swayed about on some nonexistent breeze and Rochester bled from shallow wounds, carved by his own nails unlike whatever had slaughtered the Mayor.

Despite the pain he must have been in, Rochester was smiling.

He locked eyes with Sinclair when he came in and opened his blood-soaked mouth.

With a look of pure lunacy splayed across his face, Rochester began to laugh and bounce around on the bench, gargling blood and acting like he was choking to death in an obscene mimicry of what must have been Bellman's last moments.

# CLEAN UP, AISLE MAIN STREET

"GODDAMN IT, somebody better get some goddamn answers for me in the next ten goddamn seconds or every single one of you is gonna be fired and I'll come up with new goddamn lame brained idiots to push papers all day for half of what I pay you." Johnny screamed as he paced in a circle around the crime scene, not really threatening anybody specifically, but just angry. So angry.

Sinclair understood.

It had taken them the better part of an hour, but they had finally gotten the Mayor down from the tree, and the damage was so much worse than it had appeared when Bellman was still strung up overhead.

All of the cuts the killer had made to access his innards were short, quick, violent strikes. Varying depths. Varying lengths. He had been cut open by a novice. Torn to pieces with some micro-blade, little by little, until the killers got to whatever they had been looking for. Thirty-seven different tendons and ligaments had been pulled through Bellman's skin, stretched to serve as the metaphoric puppet strings in the road display. Cleese had found a fucking fishing hook buried in the former mayor's small intestines.

"Why was there a fishing hook?"

Nobody had a satisfactory answer, but Johnny had bagged up the rusted utensil and stashed it and labeled it as the only real piece of evidence from the crime scene.

"How do you suppose a person got into those trees with a dead body and managed to hang ol' Seamus up like that?

The officers all pondered the question for a minute, looking at the thick branches of the trees, considering how high up you had to go to reach the first climbable branches.

"Seems like somebody would have needed a ladder," Cleese offered.

"Seems like multiple somebodies would have needed a ladder. No way in hell anyone pulls this off alone."

"Especially when the guy who did it was locked up all night. No way to climb the tree when you're behind bars."

"You think this was Rochester? How the shit would that work?"

"No clue, but you saw the way he was acting in that holding cell. He knew this happened. And how the hell would he know about it if he didn't have a hand in it?"

"That's circumstantial. No way does it hold up in court. Especially not when we know nobody came in or out or talked to him all yesterday or all last night."

"Nobody except the Mayor."

"What are you suggesting he did this to himself?"

"No, of course not. I'm not an idiot. It's just a weird circumstance is all."

Sinclair moved away from the other officers, tired of their aimless blathering. The other three had no clue what had happened, or how. He had a sneaking suspicion they all knew *why*, but he wasn't in the town's good graces enough to be trusted with that information. Not yet. Hopefully this would inspire Johnny to fill Sinclair in on whatever it was the town was hiding, because there was clearly *something*. But he wouldn't do it in front of Tweedle Dum or Tweedle Dee.

Patience. He would get his answers eventually. For now, though, Sinclair opted to actually investigate the trees, instead of just glancing at them stupidly, the way the other officers had.

The sides of the trees had been shredded. Hundreds of lacerations criss-crossed the bark, similar to the way the Mayor's skin. Tiny grooves had been notched in the wood as if something small had created hand or footholds for themselves, and a few of the smaller branches had been torn away, discarded in the tall grass underfoot. Something had climbed the tree, clearly.

But what?

Sinclair reached out towards the grooves, found them way too small for his fingers to get any sort of a grip in.

A kid, then?

Barker Davis, covered in blood, flashed across Sinclair's mind. Maybe this was revenge. Maybe the kid had gone all psycho crazy, started hacking apart townspeople who he blamed for his own situation the other day. But if that was the case, then why start with the Mayor? Barker couldn't have gotten to Rochester since he was locked up, but what was the connection to Seamus Bellman? And how would Rochester have known about the kill? Barker wouldn't have been working with Rochester. Not after the trauma Rochester had cause the other day. Would he?

It didn't make sense. None of this did. Not yet.

Sinclair pulled his hand away from the tree, trying not to look at the way that the Mayor's blood covered his arms all the way up to the elbows. Getting the bastard down to street level had been gruesome business.

Johnny walked over, a bit calmer, and Cleese and O'Hare whispered to each other as he moved away. Sinclair could read the looks on their faces even if he couldn't read their lips. They were shocked by the murder. Not just by the brutality of it, but by the gravity of who had been killed, and how boldly. The golden goose had been plucked. Their friend with benefits had been bled out before the town's very eyes, and the corruption around here was about to go full Manhattan Project in the power vacuum that followed. That, or it would all die off overnight, like the Mayor had. There was no telling yet. Not without knowing how fully the Mayor had everyone else wrapped around his fingers. Or why.

Sinclair regretted not confronting the man earlier when he'd hinted at his scheming. Sure, he would have caused a scene. Would have made things difficult for Johnny. But maybe if he had been bolder then he would be looking at some answers now, instead of just the spaghetti-like mess of that sleazy bastard's innards.

"Whadda ya make of all this?" Johnny asked, his voice mostly cooled off as he adjusted his belt, his back to the other two. He glanced up the road towards where they had tried to set up enough caution tape to bar the towns-folk from the scene. But Main Street was long and flat. Bellman was high. If the good people of Hollow Hills wanted to look, they were going to find a way.

"Dunno yet, chief. But I'd bet my left ass cheek Cleese and O'Hare know more than they're letting on. For a pair of idiots, they're having a real hard time playing dumb."

"Yep. You're right about that, I'm sure. But I've gotta be careful where I apply pressure, you know? I piss off some people around town by asking the hard questions, that's one thing. I piss them off and the two of us are working doubles for the next month while we try to put this thing to bed short-staffed."

"Better to keep them close and needle them slowly?"

"Yep."

The two of them stood on the sidewalk that separated Main Street from the maples and let the moment sink in. They were willingly going to work with two people that were corrupt. Maybe the corruption didn't run deep, and they didn't have hard evidence of it, but still . . . it felt too much like Charlotte again. Felt too much like everything Johnny had worked so hard to get away from; like everything Sinclair was trying to forget about.

"Well. Coroner should be here in the next hour or so. I'll make those two ass-hats do the waiting around for them. Whadda you say me and you go knock on some doors? Somebody's gotta let the rest of the Bellmans know about this, and there's a buncha houses between here and there. Gotta be somebody that saw something. You don't just move a body around like this without drawing attention . . . right?"

Sinclair shrugged.

"You want to tell the family? I'll go question Rochester?"

"Rochester was in his cell all last night and all day yesterday. No way he had a hand in this."

"Maybe he was working with somebody?"

"You must not get how ostracized that loon was from the rest of Hollow Hills if you're asking that question."

"Maybe not, but he clearly knows something. The way he was acting when I walked in?"

"Yep. Again, you're probably right, but we know where he is. He's not going anywhere anytime soon. We'll circle back to him later on. Come on, I'd rather have backup with me for this."

Sinclair sighed and nodded. As much as he thought it was important to talk to Rochester right away, to be honest, the thought of being in the station alone with the mad man was discomforting. Going with Johnny would be the safer option, even if he was convinced it wouldn't be half as productive.

The pair of them told Cleese and O'Hare what the plan was, and then Sinclair drove Johnny's truck the rest of the way into town and parked in front of the station. They went inside to wash the blood from their hands.

Rochester watched them from his cell. The man was still

covered in his own blood, having ignored the wash rags and clean clothes which Johnny had thrown to him before leaving. He stared up at the front windows of the Sheriff's Station, locking eyes with Sinclair and smiling, smiling, smiling back at him with that maddening crimson grin.

Sinclair turned away from the sight and jumped back into Johnny's truck, disgusted, confused, and more than a bit shaken.

# INTERROGATIONS

**EVEN THOUGH JOHNNY** and Sinclair spent the rest of the day making the rounds, nothing new developed from their efforts. Mrs. Bellman was awake and nursing a splitting headache when they arrived. She claimed she had fallen out of bed and was clearly covering for some abuse which she thought her husband had committed until Johnny broke the bad (good?) news that Seamus was dead. Then she spilled everything. She had been lying in bed the night before when she heard somebody moving around in the darkness. She had thought it was one of her kids, so she hadn't been too disturbed until the pillow came down over her face and something hard and heavy clunked her near the left temple.

She showed the officers her bruise, mostly hidden by her huge, curly hair. Now that he was dead, Mrs. Bellman had no qualms explaining that Seamus had hit her on occasion, when she embarrassed him in public, and although the now Ms. Bellman couldn't remember doing anything overtly bad over the last couple of weeks, she had taken Seamus' absence that morning as proof that he was mad at her, wasn't even going to talk to her about whatever had enraged him.

Sinclair took notes about all of this and Johnny got Claudia Bellman the number for a help hotline that she could call. But she hardly seemed broken up about the news of her husband's death. If anything, had that been relief?

Johnny and Sinclair left the Ms. with instructions to swing by the station later after she had informed her kids about the "tragedy", and she had agreed.

The two officers had then stopped by every single house in between the Bellmans and the crime scene to see if people had noticed something strange happening the previous night.

But no, nobody saw anything, even though the Conrads said their dog went ballistic around 4:00 in the morning for no good reason. Maybe that was a clue for their timeline. Maybe one of the Davis family's peacocks had wandered through the back yard and spooked the dog. Who knew. But Sinclair took note of it.

Cleese called when they were about halfway through the house calls. The coroners had arrived, bagged and tagged everything, and were heading back to the city to run some real tests on the corpse. They'd let Johnny know if anything interesting turned up.

This all sounded good, fine, and routine to Johnny, and as he hung up his phone and leaned against his driver's door, Sinclair decided to speak up and come clean about the day before.

"I think we need to go check the Rochester Residence again. I don't know if I was really so thorough yesterday," he said, and cringed, expecting Johnny to blow up in his face for sloppy work. But Johnny wouldn't hear anything about it.

"We cleared that place. Buncha dead goats. You said so yourself."

"I think they were lambs, but yeah. Still. There might have been a couple of rooms that I missed."

"Would a room have snuck into the Mayor's room last night and kidnapped him?"

"No, but obviously not, asshole. But there might have been something in the rooms that could tell us which way to look."

"We don't need to go back to that house yet. Not until we've fried all the other, bigger fish we've got on our plates."

Sinclair gave up. He had at least admitted his error to Johnny, so he felt better about himself. But Johnny not caring made him feel strange. Doing 90% of a job shouldn't be acceptable. He should be reprimanded for leaving, not clearing the scene. Especially with a man dead now. Johnny's laissez faire attitude was concerning.

"Get in the car. We're gonna go pay the Gattis family a visit."

"The Gattises?"

"Lumber Mill family, remember?"

"Why are we going to see them?"

Johnny paused for a minute and seemed to start a hundred different answers before settling on: "Call it an educated hunch. Biggest political guy around here politically drops dead out of nowhere, I'd kind of like to know what the biggest business guy around here thinks about that."

Sinclair didn't like that. Johnny knew more than he was letting on. And secrets between friends, especially at a moment like this, felt dangerous. But then, who was Sinclair to talk? He thought back to the book of spells he had found in Rochester's house. The one that was still in his bathroom, unrevealed to Johnny. He'd flipped through the pages again last night and tried to parse out more details from Gregory Rochester's blocky, clumsy handwriting as he fantasized about seeing Claire and Max again. He really needed to tell his boss about the book; really needed to sacrifice his own ridiculous fantasies for the sake of the case.

"I think we should go back and talk to Rochester again . . . " he said instead, still pointing the finger at Gregory, still conveniently avoiding mentioning why.

"Seriously. Sinclair. Get off him. We've got him locked up and we need to focus our attention on the people that could still be burning evidence in their back yards. Priorities, Sin. Priorities."

All he had to do was mention the book. Mention the evidence. He could redirect Johnny's investigation. But Sinclair shut up. Johnny had his mind made up, apparently. And who knew, maybe the lumber tycoon could shed some light on Rochester without Sinclair having to sacrifice the book. Wouldn't that be perfect?

"Fine. Okay. Let's go talk to the lumber mill people, if that's really what you think is right. I've just got . . . a bad feeling in my gut . . . about Rochester. Like if we leave him stewing in that cell for too long, he's gonna come back to bite us."

Gods, why couldn't Sinclair just TELL JOHNNY about the book?

He knew it was because telling him would mean he would take it. And if Johnny took it, then the chances for Sinclair to see his family again went out the window. Not that those chances really existed anyhow. Magic wasn't real. Magic wasn't real. Magic wasn't real. Sinclair kept screaming the words in his own head, but for whatever reason, he couldn't quite convince himself to believe them. Something big was happening here. Something bigger than he could rationally explain. So, he would keep the book hidden for a little while longer. Just in case.

"Noted," Johnny said, interrupting Sinclair's thoughts. "And I'll let you go check that house out again tomorrow if it'll ease your mind. For today I just want to round up any other threads we can find. We good?"

"Yeah. We're good."

"Thanks, Sin. I'm glad you're here for this. Dunno what I'd be doing with the Mayor dead and just Cleese and O'Hare running around covering their own asses from whatever's happening. It feels good to have somebody I can trust."

Sinclair smiled at that, even though he didn't let Johnny see the look.

Being commended, being valued, it warmed a little part of Sinclair's soul which he had thought dead. From the depths of his depression, something like self-worth began to simmer again.

Moving out here was beginning to work. It was under the most insane of circumstances, but for the first time in months, Sinclair felt his shoulders rise a little higher, saw a sense of purpose begin to materialize in front of him. There was a road from ruin out here after all. It was just a shame the road had been paved with Seamus Bellman's blood.

Johnny threw the truck in gear and turned towards the Gattis Lumber Mill.

# TIMBER

**THE GATTIS LUMBER MILL** was enormous. Multiple stories high with a forest green roof and vertical, dark wood paneling, it blended into the trees around it, tricking the eye into thinking that the whole woods had sworn allegiance to the structure, which was a great grand irony, Sinclair thought grimly.

The mill backed up to a wide, but slow-moving river which wound down from the mountain and which loggers in the past had used to float their trees to the mill for processing. But the soft hiss and gargle of flowing water was drowned out by the scream of the saw blades inside. The air was full of the piney smells of freshly cut wood and the sawdust everywhere created a tan haze above the mill like a miniature sandstorm was descending upon Hollow Hills.

Johnny opened a tackle box in the back of his truck which had goggles, earplugs, and masks inside, all certainly placed there for trips to this place. He handed a set to Sinclair before pulling his own gear on and wading into the throngs of workers who were all equipped similarly, moving purposefully back and forth, into and out of the establishment like worker bees around their hive.

Johnny led the way to a side door and the offices which were situated at the opposite end of the mill from the massive awnings where the main work was taking place. They passed a worker who Sinclair was fairly sure was Mr. Barker, the peacock farmer, exiting the building quickly, and he made eye contact with the Sheriff, pushed past, and immediately grabbed the walkie talkie from the belt at his hip.

It was impossible to hear what Mr. Barker said through the sawmills and the ear plugs, but Johnny picked up his pace. The Gattises would know they were here now, if they hadn't been alerted the minute their truck pulled up.

Inside the noise died down a bit. Enough that Sinclair felt

comfortable taking his ear plugs out, but not quiet enough for "inside voices" to be heard.

Sinclair looked around at the small, but lavishly furnished reception area. A young, pretty receptionist sat at a beautiful red wood desk, typing away in front of three computer monitors. A headset was on her head, pressing her brown hair down, and she was speaking in some strange Eastern European sounding language until she noticed the officers, said her goodbyes, typed a couple last notes, and then hung up with the client.

She turned towards Johnny.

"Welcome, officer. What can the Gattis Family Mill do for you today?" The words slipped out smoothly, any hint of the brusque accent the woman had been using a moment before totally dissipated in a flash, the sign of a practiced linguist. Sinclair was impressed.

"We're here to talk to Mr. Gattis for a few minutes, if he's available."

"Oh. Sorry. Mr. Gattis has a remarkably busy schedule today. If you could wait, I could maybe get you some time on Friday."

The receptionist turned towards one of her screens as if meaning to check on her boss's schedule. But she knew, and Johnny and Sinclair knew, that it was just an act.

"Ma'am. This is police business. We really need to see Mr. Gattis now."

"I am sorry, but Mr. Gattis was very clear that nobody was to interrupt him today unless they were on the schedule. If you had a warrant-"

Johnny's groan cut the secretary off.

"You're really gonna make us go get a warrant just to have a talk with your employer."

"Or you could come back on Friday."

"Ma'am, what's your name?"

"Woah! Woah! Woah!" a voice from the back hallway interrupted. A large man with a thick but short beard appeared in the doorway to the reception area, the coffee in his bear-like hands still steaming. The man smiled at everybody, especially the receptionist, and acted carefree and laid back despite the way Johnny had begun raising his voice, and the sudden appearance of two members of the Sheriff's department at his place of business. His smile was disarming, his calm demeanor infectious.

He reminded Sinclair painfully of the late Mayor Bellman.

"What's all the hub-ub about in here? Shannon, are you giving our guests a hard time? You know the Sheriff's always welcome to come talk to me!"

The secretary looked flustered.

"But you said . . . " Shannon let the thought trail off and shook her head. She dropped back into her seat and began clicking at the screens around her, muttering something under her breath as the mill's owner sauntered over towards Johnny, threw a big arm across his shoulders.

"Sorry about her. Been talking to her for weeks about how to filter my workload some. Might have drilled the idea too deep into her ol' noggin if you know what I mean."

Sinclair didn't, but Mr. Gattis' choice of wording gave him a weird feeling in his gut.

As if sensing Sinclair's discomfort, Gattis spun on his heel to face Sinclair, pulling Johnny around with him.

"And who's young buck here? Folks said you got a new pup running around the station. I just suspected he would be bigger. Get some muscle to help you round yer crooks up. If you want, I've got some brawny types around here. You can fire Mr. Twig-man and get some real muscle."

Gattis winked at Sinclair as if they were good buddies who ribbed on each other all the time. Sinclair didn't appreciate the jokes though. He took a step back and tried to keep his face neutral, burying his scowl in his clenched fists and gritted teeth. He stole a glance at Johnny, to see if his boss would stand up for him, but no luck.

"This is Sinclair Redman," Johnny said. He ducked out from under Gattis' arm and re-straightened his uniform, then just completely ignored the remarks about Sinclair. "I'm afraid we're here with some bad news, Mr. Gattis."

"Jeeze-us. Don't come in here with that 'Mr. Gattis' stuff. Ethan. You know to call me Ethan."

"Fine then. *Ethan.* We have some unfortunate news that might be best told to you in your office, if you can spare a minute."

"Course I can, son. Come on back. You want coffee? Shannon over there makes a good damn cup. It ain't half as bitter as she can be, promise."

Shannon threw her boss a look that could have killed, then she plastered the fakest, most forced smile imaginable across her face as she nodded.

"No thanks. No coffee. We've already been by Mama Jean's," Johnny lied. Sinclair approved. He wouldn't have trusted the coffee from around here. The way Ethan Gattis had faked being surprised to hear the Sheriffs in his reception area, despite Barker's warning, coupled with Shannon's stand-offish reception had Sinclair's senses on red alert. These people were putting on a show. What were they hiding? Sinclair had no clue, yet. But he knew he shouldn't trust them.

He followed Johnny and Ethan down the hall, making a point to glance backwards frequently, checking his six and staying on his toes. Ahead of him, Gattis tried to make way-too-friendly of a conversation with Johnny. It set Sinclair on edge a little bit, hearing how chummy this potential criminal was with the Sheriff of Hollow Hills. Sinclair knew Johnny was above corruption. After all the shit they'd waded through in Charlotte, there was no way a small-town lumber miller like Gattis had pulled the wool over his boss's eyes . . . was there?

"Ain't nothing in this world better than the smell of some fresh cut pine first thing in the morning, you know?" Gattis was saying. "Gotta find a way to bottle that shit up. Sell it like a cologne. We'd double our profits overnight. Everybody in town getting laid when the women can't keep their hands off us."

"Mr. Gattis-"

"-Ethan."

"Ethan. We've got a serious matter to discuss." Johnny tried to tone down the conversation as they reached the crude lumber titan's office and waited for him to find the proper key to unlock the door.

"Probably shouldn't be telling you company advancement plans anyhow. Next thing I know you'll open your own cologne shop."

"No danger of that, sir."

"But there is danger, isn't there?"

Gattis pushed the door open and gave Johnny and Sinclair a mischievous look, as if he already knew about the Bellman murder. His eyes twinkled with excitement as he waved the officers into his office and closed the door behind them. Sinclair listened to make sure he didn't lock it.

The room was enormous, far larger than any office needed to be. To their right a long, dark, wooden table was surrounded by eight high-backed chairs, each carved from matching stained timber. Gattis settled himself into the one differentiated chair out of the set, twice as high backed as the others with fancy arm rests, the chair was more akin to a throne than any real comfortable seating arrangement. And yet Gattis seemed right at home in it, leaning forward, setting his elbows on the table and clasping his hands in front of him.

"So. We're in here now. Away from my secretary and my workers. Can I hear this bad news you referenced now? Take a seat. Make yourselves comfortable."

Johnny did, but Sinclair stayed on his feet near the door. Gattis raised an eyebrow at this, but said nothing, turning his attention instead towards Johnny.

"It's about Mayor Bellman. He's . . . dead. To say the least. We found his body this morning."

Gattis' face curled downward gently, as if he was tasting something he disliked. But he didn't really look 'surprised' or 'upset.' Sinclair quietly tested the door handle nearby, found that it turned easily, came unlatched with a little pressure. He made sure he could remember all the turns to get back to the receptionist's area.

"Well now. That's a shame. Truly. It is," Gattis said after a prolonged pause.

"Sure is." Johnny said back.

"So you came here as a courtesy call because . . . what? Bellman and I weren't the closest of friends. But surely you must have known that? I know you're still a bit green around the gills here, but surely you've picked up on THAT in the last three years, Sheriff."

Johnny didn't react. Like Sinclair, he was trying to read Gattis's reactions. It was an interrogation without officially being an interrogation. Maybe he would slip up. Reveal that he knew more about the death than Johnny had told him about.

"But no. You're not here because of that. You're what? Looking out for my business? Maybe you think just because he's got money and I've got some money, we must be . . . have been . . . connected somehow? A pair of oligarchs overseeing the town? Well sorry to disappoint you there, Sheriff, but our connections were only ever in passing. He passed the laws that let my mill stay open and trade effectively, I supplied jobs to most of his constituents. End of story. Unless there's something else you're trying to imply?"

"No. Just figured you'd be interested in hearing the news before your workers did. I imagine it'll be all they're talking about at the water cooler by tomorrow. Some folk might need a mental health day or something with their beloved mayor found dead and all. Think of this more as a courtesy call than anything else."

Gattis snickered.

"Mental health day. God, that bullshit's gonna be the death of America. But fine. I get your point. And I appreciate the, uh, the courtesy call, as you phrased it. But now I've got a busy day ahead of me. Especially with the threat of my workers not showing up tomorrow cause they've got a case of the feel bads. Gotta try to drain that labor out of 'em today. The papers haven't gotten a hold of it yet?"

"Not that I know of."

"Well aren't I special then?"

Johnny blew some air through his nose, rose from his seat and looked around at his expensive surroundings. It really was impressive how much money a lumber mill could generate. Strangely impressive.

The juxtaposition between this place and the rest of the town didn't sit right with Sinclair. Really, nothing did about the Gattis Mill at this point. He wanted to get out. Right away. If Bellman had made Sinclair feel gross and uncomfortable when they were in the station, Sinclair couldn't put into words how much his skin was crawling at being *in* this viper's den.

He nudged the door open. Despite the size of the room, somehow it felt like the walls were too close. Sinclair's sight lines were obstructed. There were no windows in the room, so there was no telling what all of Gattis's workers were doing at the moment. Maybe Shannon had tipped them off. Maybe they were cutting the brake lines of Johnny's truck, setting a trap for the officers who had dared to look too closely into their place of business. If Bellman's death was Gattis' fault, instead of Rochester's like Sinclair had assumed, then they would have walked straight into the crosshairs here.

Johnny must have felt similarly, based on the way he back-pedaled towards Sinclair, never taking his eyes off Gattis who still sat comfortably, unphased atop his throne.

“Well then. Thanks for your time, Mr. Gattis.”

“Ethan.”

“Yep. Sure. You take care, and good luck tomorrow. I imagine having a bunch of distracted, daydreaming hands around a lumber mill may lead to an issue or two.”

“By the way, boys. You picked up Gregory Rochester the other day, right?”

Sinclair paused at that, already halfway out the door.

He and Johnny both turned to study Gattis’ face. Gattis just smiled back at them, a slim, devilish smirk.

“I’m assuming you still have him locked away? Probably in that little drunk-tank of yours? Is he alone in there still? Safely tucked away from the rest of us?”

Johnny didn’t answer. Just stared back.

“That’s good. Lotta people around here gonna assume this was his fault. Lotta good folk around here are gonna be looking for revenge for their fallen mayor after what Rochester did to him.”

“We never said he was murdered.”

“No. I suppose you didn’t. Still. Healthy young buck like the mayor doesn’t just drop dead out of nowhere does he? Can’t help but assume there’s some foul play afoot. Especially with the election coming up, this really throws a wrench in some things, huh? I’m gonna go out on a limb here and say that . . . this . . . ” he gestured around him with his hands. “Whatever this is. It probably isn’t over yet, is it Sheriff? You might want to keep your gun close. Might want to surround yourself with . . . ” the mill owner really looked at Sinclair for the first time . . . “people who you can actually trust. Elsewise these things tend to spin out of control. Trust me on that one.”

“Is that a threat?”

“Of course not. I wouldn’t be so stupid. Lets instead consider it, oh how did you phrase it, *common courtesy*?”

Gattis stopped just short of telling on himself. His dimples stayed creased exactly the same, his smile calm, but his eyes twinkled with a wild roguish energy. He knew more than he was letting on. But how? And what?

“Been a while since we had any major accidents around here. Not like this. Not since before you arrived, huh, Sheriff? But you know what they say. Sometimes when it rains it pours.”

Johnny and Sinclair stayed put for a long while, but Gattis

offered nothing else. No more cryptic hints about what he may or may not be privy to.

Sinclair placed a hand on his boss's shoulder and pulled him away. When they got back to the truck, Sinclair took an extra moment to inspect it; to make sure nothing was ticking, dripping, or swaying differently than it should have been. But all seemed fine. Just like it always did around Hollow Hills, there was a perfect facade of tranquility.

The engine started without issue, and the pair drove away from the Gattis Lumber Mill none the wiser, but even more on edge than they had been when they arrived.

As they pulled closer to town, Johnny's phone began to blow up. They must have been in a dead zone around the lumber mill. Now, its signal found fresh, Johnny's cell screamed for attention, alerting him about all the texts, messages, and phone calls about all the things that had gone wrong in his and Sinclair's absence.

# WRITING ON THE WALL

**BACK AT THE STATION**, Sinclair made a beeline for the showers. Between the bloody mess that morning and the sawmill he felt grimy and disgusting. This was the second time Sinclair had found himself dripping blood, and he didn't appreciate the trend. Seeing Rochester in his cell, body still oozing crimson from his self-inflicted scratches only served to emphasize his feeling.

"I need a minute, Johnny," he said, and Johnny nodded, understood.

"Yeah. Take your time. Clear your head."

Johnny said the words without looking at Sinclair. He was headed straight to his office, eyes locked on Rochester who was sitting quietly in his cell.

"We should probably call a doc over for that asshole, huh?" Johnny mumbled, almost to himself.

Sinclair shrugged, uncaring.

"Sure, I guess. He seems fine though. Like, weirdly fine. As if none of the mornings events had happened at all. As if the streaks of red which criss-crossed all of his exposed skin were perfectly natural, his place in a holding cell entirely natural. As Sinclair studied the captive, Rochester turned his head slowly and smiled.

In the back of the station, Johnny's door clicked shut.

"You should take a picture, officer. It'll last longer."

Sinclair startled at the sound of the man's voice. He had been silent for so long . . .

"Have you boys gotten the mayor all cleaned up yet?"

"How do you know something happened to the mayor?" Sinclair questioned back. Nobody had told Rochester what had happened. Nobody had even mentioned it yet. He had intentionally avoided specifics until they were out of the station earlier. O'Hare and Cleese were still at the crime scene waiting for the body to get picked up . . . weren't they? There was no way that Rochester, locked in his cell here, could have heard about the crime. Certainly there was no way he could know that the victim was the mayor.

Rochester's smile expanded from a slim grin into a full-toothed gash across his face. His teeth were stained red and dripping with his own blood.

"Don't doubt what I know, boy. I know lots of things. Lots and lots and lots and lots and lots and . . . lots . . . of things." He wrapped his arms around himself in a sort of self-embrace.

Despite every instinct, Sinclair stepped closer to the holding cell.

"How are you doing this?"

Rochester cocked his head to the side at an obscene angle, as if he were a doll with a screw loose in his neck.

"Wrong question."

"No, I'm pretty damn sure I asked the right question."

"What you really want to know is why, officer. The 'how' is just a mechanism. Hinges and gears to drive the story forward. You don't really care how a car drives. You don't really care about 'how' a tire gains traction or 'how' an engine turns four wheels. All you care about is that the car is moving, and where it's headed. Where it's coming from. Is the car driving towards a collapsing bridge? Or away from it? And if a car is barreling forward, driving towards its own destruction, then isn't the 'why' so much more interesting than the 'how'?"

Sinclair's head was entirely spun around now.

"The hell are you talking about? You know what? Fine. WHY, then. Why are you doing this?"

Sinclair wanted so badly to crane his neck around, to check what Johnny was up to. Did he see that their prisoner was actually, finally talking? Sinclair needed backup. He needed a recording device. He needed all of this random nonsense that Rochester was spewing to be documented somehow, and yet he knew that if he broke eye contact from the suspect, the spell would be broken. If he looked away, moved away, changed any little thing about this moment, then Rochester would retreat back into his own head again.

"Why?" Rochester repeated the word as if Sinclair had surprised him by asking. "Why, why, why?" The word got repeated as the record in Rochester's head skipped. Rochester's green eyes shone with the same life that Gattis' eyes had back at the lumber mill.

"I know how much you've lost, Mr. Redford," Rochester finally said, breaking out of his trance. "Beatrice told me all about your wife. Your child. So much pain. So much sorrow."

Sinclair felt his heart drop into his stomach.

"The fuck did you just say?"

Rochester blinked and looked away, seemingly forgetting that Sinclair was in the room with him. He stared instead at a dark corner of the station, behind Sinclair, away from Johnny's office. He seemed to address his words towards the shadows.

"Yes. I know about the fire. But maybe that's your 'why.' Maybe that fire is the reason you're driving your car towards the collapsing bridge. That's what Claire thinks. She wants you to turn your car around, Officer."

Sinclair turned to his right, following Rochester's gaze to the dark corner of the room where a small figure stood, watching them.

" . . . Max . . . ?" he questioned, but he knew it was him. He would have recognized his son anywhere.

In his cell behind Sinclair, Rochester fell silent.

"Max. Come here, buddy. How did you . . . ? How are you . . . ?" Sinclair couldn't finish his thoughts; he was too overwhelmed by the impossibility of the moment. He took a tentative step forward, his hands trembling.

The doll in the corner came into view slowly. Not Max, but an eerily similar facsimile of him; the same height, the same frame, its hair the same chestnut color, falling in a messy mop atop his head with the same cowlick in the back. Its face had been painted the same shade as Max's skin had been before the flames charred him black.

The dolls' eyes stared back at Sinclair, brown and doe-ey.

"Son of a bitch."

"I'm so sorry," Rochester whispered behind him. Then the mad man laid down on his steel bench and turned his nose towards the wall, apparently done talking to Sinclair. Sinclair scowled at the man, then crossed the room and crouched in front of the doll.

Shit, even its clothes reminded Sinclair of the clothes Max used to wear: basketball shorts and a sports top, as if he was always ready to jump into the next big game.

With another distrusting glance back at Rochester, then a scan towards Johnny who was locked in, focused on something on his computer screen, Sinclair stepped back from the doll.

This wasn't right.

He was losing his mind. Max wasn't here. Max was dead. Sinclair had put him to rest back in Charlotte, confirmed his death in the morgue and watched his casket get lowered into the gaping maw of the Earth.

He didn't know how this doll got here. He didn't understand how it looked so similar to Max. But he forced himself not to care. He had to leave the past in the past. He had to turn the car around. Get off the collapsing bridge. Whatever it was that Rochester had said, Sinclair felt like he understood. Sort of. Gods, how far gone was he, finding motivation in the nonsensical ramblings of a mass murderer.

Sinclair turned on his heel, spinning away from the doll. He had half a mind to go straight into Johnny's office, to tell him everything that just happened, but no.

It was too insane. Too weird. He'd just sound like an idiot if he went in there trying to tell Johnny that Rochester had seen Claire, or that there was some strange doll that a kid left in the station, and that it looked just like Max. Johnny would dismiss it all with a roll of his eyes.

And besides, something about Johnny was off.

Sinclair still needed that shower. Maybe a couple minutes under the hot water would help him to make sense of what was happening. Maybe he could explain it all to Johnny once he could explain it to himself. The book. The doll. The fact that the ghosts of his past were still literally popping up all around him, confounding an already absurd investigation. Maybe he needed to be excused from this case.

He marched past Rochester's holding cell, casting a look at the bloody mess of a man. Still suspicious, but now, Sinclair felt a rising sense of curiosity, of sympathy. But how, or . . . WHY, Rochester was doing what he was doing, Sinclair still had no clue.

# RAINING BLOOD

**GATTIS RETURNED HOME** that night just before sun down.

Those fuckers from the Sheriff's department had ruined his entire day. Not because of the Bellman news. He had already heard about that from Jennings who drove past the scene earlier in the morning, had called Gattis like a good little soldier, and who had driven away like he was supposed to. No, Bellman's death was an inconvenience, but it was an inconvenience that Gattis knew how to handle.

What had really jacked up his operation was the cops coming, stepping foot on his property for the first time in over a year, and spooking the shit out of his workers.

"Nobody tell the cooks!" he had emphasized over and over and fucking *over* when Barker warned him about the Sheriff's arrival on their walkie talkie. And what had Barker done? He'd blabbed to the rest of the grunts who had let it slip to the cooks that the authorities were snooping around. So while the saw mill kept whirring away overhead, down in the basement, production on the Gattis Family Mill's real primary export ground to a painful, paranoid, screeching halt. Two of the smoke stacks which belched their fumes into the open air above Hollow Hills fell stagnant, and it was a damn good thing the Sheriff didn't know what he was looking at while he was poking about.

Gattis didn't give a shit about the Mayor. Sure, they had a decent working relationship with each other. Gattis would shuttle some 'anonymous' campaign donations into the mayor's pocket, and in exchange the mayor would help make sure that the meth crisis in their fair town stayed swept under the rug, a back-burner issue that never really gathered too much attention. Not directly.

But political stooges were a dime a dozen. Whoever the next

mayor was, Gattis could grease their palms just the same as he had greased Bellman's.

But he had just lost an entire day's production, and now all of his 'special' employees were going to be walking on egg-shells, regardless of how many times Gattis reassured them that Johnny and Sinclair knew nothing about their operations. They would want extra safety precautions. They would demand raises. If the Sheriff was going to just come snooping around unannounced, they would all claim that the risk to them had increased, and workers always wanted to be compensated for added risk.

It was all going to be a massive headache for Gattis.

Not to mention dealing with Gattis' contact in Raleigh who had been expecting a shipment to arrive by the end of the week. Gattis would have to find some way to compensate him also, for the delay.

Gattis slammed the door of his truck shut, drawing the smallest bit of satisfaction from the way the sound echoed through the trees and mountains surrounding his lakeside estate. If Gregory Rochester's hobbled-together shack was on the 'outskirts' of town, then Gattis lived all the way off the opposite end of the map. He didn't want to see the people of Hollow Hills, ever, when he wasn't at work. In truth, they all disgusted him. Swine content to live bare-minimum existences, with no aspirations to become anything more than a small-town nobody. He hired the town because they served no threat to him. Teach them how to do bland labor: measure the chemicals, check the hypo phosphorous acid levels, introduce water at the right time. It was all utterly mindless, and as long as Gattis kept the laborers divided, each seeing just one step to the process, then Gattis' employees didn't have the intelligence to realize that half their jobs at the mill had no connection whatsoever to the milling process.

But dealing with idiots was a delicate process. And today that process had been thrown out of balance.

He took the steps to his house one at a time, not in any rush to get indoors. He never found himself in much of a rush. Rushing caused mistakes. Mistakes drew attention. Attention bred threats.

He opened his screen door, the heavy oak door, the first plank of wood his mill had ever cut under his care, hung wide open, the day's temperature far too pleasant to be barred outside. Every window to the house had been thrown as wide as could be, and the heaters and the air conditioning all sat blissfully silent. In the living room to Gattis's right, an oversized fan spun lazily in a circle. Everything seemed perfectly fine and natural. His issues from the mill that day hadn't followed him home and his sanctuary remained untainted. Or so it seemed at first.

Darlin', I'm home," he called into the empty cavern of his abode, unaware of what lay within.

There was no response. But that wasn't completely unusual. The late afternoon air sat so heavy and still that it seemed to encourage a silent lethargy. Gattis found his own eyelids drooping a bit as he walked through the house, longing to take a pre-dinner nap. Surely Martha was up in their room resting her head. Her car had been sitting outside, so Ethan knew that she must be on the premises somewhere, but he vowed to stay silent and to let her sleep. He could prepare dinner. Steaks. They would have steaks tonight. Martha didn't love red meat, but after the day Ethan'd had, if he was going to cook, then he was going to make what he wanted.

He entered the kitchen, opened the fridge, and grabbed a few cuts of meat and a Budweiser. They were rich enough to afford any beers that they wanted, but Gattis found that a plain old Bud was his comfort drink. All the other shit they made these days were too fruity or fancy. Like the rest of the outside world, even alcohol was getting bastardized by the younger generation. Why couldn't they all just drive trucks, drink beer, and make money like real Americans?

The grill was out back. A jumbo-sized, stainless steel monster which sat on their back porch with a view that let Gattis survey the lake while the ribeye steaks that he slapped over fresh flames began to sizzle and sear. Gattis cracked the Bud open, dusted the top of the meat with salt and cracked black pepper, then leaned against the rail and thought his thoughts.

It was as he debated the pros and cons of returning to the mill tomorrow and inspiring his workers through fear versus inspiring them through confidence and reassurances that Gattis's eyes fell, distracted, towards the ripples in the lake. The slight breeze caused the surface of the water to shimmer, microscopic waves forming in the middle of the open water, then drifting closer and closer and closer to the Gattis property, unobstructed until they hit the dock and the body in the water.

Gattis snapped out of his daydreams.

Face-down, floating just to the left of his dock, a long, 6'1, tanned body bobbed up and down gently, riding the slight undulations of the rippling water the same as the rowboat on the opposite side of the dock was.

There was no mistaking the plume of blonde hair which surrounded the head, even from this distance.

"Martha!" Gattis exclaimed, dropping his grill tongs and sliding over his back deck's railing with a nimble leap which defied his age and his weight. He hustled down the back lawn, towards the shore line, frantically at first, then slower and slower.

That was Martha alright. Face down in the water. Unmoving. His lizard brain wanted to go diving into the water to save his wife, but his rational brain thought better of that. She was clearly dead. He could see spirals of red drifting through the water where her face must have been. Diving into the water wouldn't save her somehow. But this might be a trap. And if it was a trap, then haste was the enemy.

Gattis slowed to a stop, forcing down his initial burst of adrenaline. He looked left and right along the shoreline before tip-toeing onto the dock and picking up an oar from the rowboat. The long, heavy bit of wood felt good in his hands; the embodiment of security.

Gattis looked around again, grip tightening on his weapon. But he was all alone. Just him and his dead wife, floating like some discarded trash up against the edge of the lake.

Carefully, keeping an eye peeled for any sign of trouble, Ethan Gattis tried to wedge the oar under his wife's shoulder, used it and the edge of the dock as a fulcrum to try to flip her over.

It worked, and the resulting splash made Gattis jump back, away from the grotesque sight before him.

Martha Gattis was dead alright.

Her eyes had been removed, and based on the scratches which ringed each socket, the process hadn't been quick or painless. Her lips were split too far apart, the skin torn and her jaw broken in order to stretch it wide enough for a gallon baggie of the Gattis Family Mill's meth to be shoved into her throat. Two smaller bags had been crammed into her vacant eye holes.

Gattis reached a shaking hand down towards Martha's face, wanting to pull the bags free from his wife's skull, but no. Then his fingerprints would be on the bags. The lake water had probably washed away the real culprit's prints, so Gattis grabbing the bags now would leave him as the sole suspect.

He screamed, a deep, chesty bellow which made birds all the way at the top of Pine Mountain leap to the skies in terror. Gattis swung the oar down, slammed it against the edge of the dock, splitting the tool in half in his rage, then slamming the broken wood down over and over again until nothing remained in his hands except splinters and blood and anger.

Who would fucking dare . . . ?

Gattis turned and looked back towards his house where the smells of his steaks had transformed from a mouth-watering temptation to a now-it's-burning, ash-ey scent with black smoke to match. But Gattis looked past this. Suddenly every window to the house was shut. But he was positive those windows had been open when he first arrived home. Absolutely certain.

He glared at the windows. Somebody was in his house. He saw them upstairs, in his bedroom window, standing just behind the thin curtains, looking out at Gattis, at Martha, and Ethan threw all of his prior caution to the wind. He saw red in a way that he never had before and, throwing the last remaining bit of the oar to the side, he charged back up his lawn towards the back deck.

He ignored the steaks, let them burn, and broke through his back screen door rather than wasting time opening the handle. Gattis wasn't in a mindset for carefully opening and closing a latch. He wasn't in a mindset for preserving his dinner. He was hell-bent on one thing and one thing alone: destruction.

His sawed-off shotgun was still nestled under the couch, and his fingers brushed against the million dollars of cash "go money" which always sat alongside the weapon. Gattis racked a shell home, finger already on the trigger, ready to throw shot fragments into the gut of whoever that was upstairs in his bedroom.

It couldn't be the Sheriff. That yellow bastard hadn't even had the guts to come confront Gattis until today. No chance he could have ramped all the way up to scraping out a person's eyes so quickly.

And not Rochester either. Lord knew, that asshole had the motive, but he'd been locked away since yesterday. Hadn't he?

What if they were working together? What if the Sheriff had distracted Gattis at his place of work that morning while Rochester ran free, killing his wife in retribution for the 'accident' four years back?

That had to be it.

Nobody else would have had the guts to come after Gattis like this. Not in his own home. Not with his wife.

"Rochester, you half-brained, cast out, son of a bitch. You'd best kill yourself now, cause you don't want to know what I'm about to do if I get my hands on you," Gattis screamed as he took the stairs two-at-a-time.

He saw shadows shift around in the space between his bedroom door and the floor, lined up his shot, and pulled the trigger. The gunshot was deafening, the gun kicked back against Gattis' shoulder, and there was a crack. Holes ripped through the beautiful, thick mahogany at the same time as Gattis' bone fractured. But Gattis didn't slow with the pain, instead shifting to his left leg, then driving all of his weight forward, through the heel of his right boot as he kicked what was left of the door down.

Gattis shot before he looked.

The shotgun bucked backwards again, cracking Gattis' collar bone fully, but hurling buckshot through the bedroom like hellfire, shredding Gattis' bed, exploding the window which Gattis had seen the killer looking through earlier, and toppling over the . . . mannequin . . . which had been positioned in the middle of the room's centerpiece rug.

It had been a trap. Again. The mannequin in the window. Martha's killer had to have known about Gattis's short temper, lured him up here, been hiding somewhere else on the main landing. If the killer had been in any other room in the house, Gattis would have stormed right past them, and now they'd have an open shot at his back.

As if reading Gattis's thoughts, something hard, sharp, and heavy slammed into Ethan Gattis' back, splitting through four of his upper right ribs, and dropping him instantly to the floor.

Face down, blinded by pain, Gattis remained vaguely aware of something, no, some *things* clacking about behind him. The sound of bits of wood clapping together circled around Gattis, where he had fallen, like sharks.

Ethan tried to raise his head, to see who was doing this to him, but as he did the object in his back ripped itself free and a second wave of searing pain tore through Gattis.

He wished for death. Ethan had always thought of himself as strong and courageous, but now, facing this sort of excruciating attack, all of his stubborn resilience left him. His head lolled to the side and his eyes flitted open in time to see the mannequin, the one which had distracted him moments ago, rising from the floor.

So Ethan was delirious. He must have been. The pain was playing tricks on his mind because no way in hell was a hunk of plastic rising up, walking towards him, stepping carefully over Ethan's arm and the pool of his blood.

There was no way that had just happened. No way at all that mannequin had just stood up and walked-

Gattis felt something large, wide, and cold press against the wound in his back. Broken ribs shifted out of the way and his organs compressed and ruptured to make room for the hand that forced its way up, inside him.

Ethan Gattis's last thought was that he could feel the mannequin's forearm pressing back against his spine, his fingers wriggling their way up towards his throat. There was a crack and the mannequin shoved with inhuman strength, muscling his hand up into position in Gattis's mouth, the skin around his throat bulging and flexing to make room for the plastic knuckles.

The mannequin sat down, stiffly, on Ethan Gattis's bed as the second mannequin dragged the Mayor's body in as well, sitting next to the first mannequin. The blood on the mannequin stuck it to the comforter a bit, but neither of the mannequins cared about that. They sat their victims on their knees and, hands shoved up their prey's backs, began to work Gattis and Bellman's jaws up and down up and down. Their teeth clacked together, and if mannequins' faces were able to show any emotion, an onlooker would surely have thought they saw them laughing.

The puppet show lasted only a few minutes before the mannequins stood, apparently, bored, and proceeded to crash their dummies' heads together repeatedly, beating the men's faces to a pulp and spewing gore and chipped teeth across the bedroom floor until one man's brain matter couldn't be distinguished from the others'. The mannequins walked in sync across the room and hurled the mens' ruined corpses through the already broken window, letting the pair crash and burn onto the smoldering grill below while the mannequins began their march back to town, seeking other sinners to play with.

# RETURN TO DOLL HOUSE: ROUND 3

THE SHOWER GAVE Sinclair the clarity he had been seeking.

As he washed the grime and the blood from his hair and his hands, Sinclair knew that it was his time to take the lead on the investigation. No more just following Johnny's directions. If they were going to get any closure about what was happening here, then the answers would be in the Rochester House. Not at the Gattis Mill. Not going door to door aimlessly for hours.

Johnny was hesitating; dodging the most obvious crime scene for reasons that Sinclair couldn't quite pin down. Sinclair had allowed himself to get sidetracked by his boss, the friend he had trusted so completely back in Charlotte. Something had changed about Johnny. And Sinclair didn't want to think too hard about what that change might have been. If Johnny had been corrupted by the town, by Gattis, by Bellman, then Sinclair would have to get out of here.

But first thing was first. Sinclair needed to see this murder through. He would return to the Rochester House, discover whatever was left to be discovered there, whatever had been nagging at the back of his mind since the last time he fled. He would get the book from his house, turn it over as evidence, and bring the culprit to justice. Whatever connection was uncovered about Rochester or Johnny or Gattis or the kid, Barker, Sinclair would sort that out in the aftermath. But Rochester's accomplice, whoever, whatever they were, would be revealed once Sinclair dug through those last two rooms. He was sure of it.

He stepped from the shower and toweled off, making a point of not looking *too* directly at the ghost of his dead wife which he could sense lingering in the steam-covered mirror. She followed behind him, as she so often did, and he felt her drifting about, lurking in the edges of his vision.

"I need to turn the car around, huh? Well jokes on you. The tire's still flat."

It was the type of joke that Claire would have appreciated, had she still been alive. Stupid 'dad humor.'

He grabbed a fresh uniform off the pile in the bathroom supply closet, threw his old, blood-soaked rags straight in the hazardous waste bin, and stuffed himself into the stiff, starched new beige button-down and slacks. He held his name badge under the tap for a few seconds, working with his thumb to get the last of the Bellman blood washed from it, and then, boots in hand, Sinclair turned off the shower lights and snuck into the main floor of the Sheriff's Station. To his right, the lights in Johnny's office were all turned on, and Johnny sat with his back to Sinclair, slouched forward, phone pressed against his ear. The chief's office was soundproof, but even from behind, Sinclair could read his friend's frustrated, angry body language. Whatever phone call was happening, it wasn't going well.

Sinclair used the distraction to his advantage. He didn't turn any extra lights on in the station, just snuck through with his head down low, tip-toeing on socks that barely made a whisper, past the holding cell. Rochester smiled at Sinclair as he passed and held a scabbed, gnarled finger up to his lips, whispering "Shhhh," his eyes glittering with insanity.

Sinclair ignored the way the crazy man crept alongside him in his cell, instead focusing on opening his desk slowly, pulling out the spare keys without jangling them, and slipping out the front door to the station without drawing any extra attention to himself.

The truck started easily, and Sinclair waited until he had backed the vehicle out and gotten halfway up the road before he turned the headlights on. He would text Johnny in a bit, tell him that he had left to get a bite to eat. Ask him if he wanted anything. Johnny wouldn't think twice about it, but Sinclair hadn't wanted to be stopped and questioned on his way out the door. Until he knew exactly why Johnny was being so cagey, he wanted to be acting first, talking second. His fear from that first day at the station welled back up. When Mayor Bellman had tried to sell his snake oil to Sinclair, when Sinclair had asked Johnny, point blank, if he was entangled in some bullshit and when Johnny had said, point blank back, that he wasn't.

"Damn it, old buddy. How deep are you?" Sinclair whispered under his breath. The truck coasted along Hollow Hills' back roads until Sinclair drove past the hanging tree which Johnny had shown him on day one. Had Johnny been trying to scare him back then? Or was there something else about this place, about Rochester, which Johnny had known about, had tried to draw Sinclair's attention to without really drawing attention to it. Those first days had been such a strange blur. Between the peacock farm and the doll tree, the Mayor's sleaziness and the Lumber Mill, it seemed Sinclair was trying to make sense of too many pieces to too many different puzzles. What was important here? What wasn't? And what was he still missing? Because even if he ignored the peacocks, the crazy toymaker, the naked, mutilated corpse, the pieces remaining still had no binding agent. No clear motive.

Some bullshit was occurring, and Sinclair had no clue why.

Maybe if he could find that motive, then all the other puzzle pieces could just be ignored. He could cut this chaos off at the source.

The headlights found the Rochester House just as forsaken and ramshackle as Sinclair had left it, with even the door still hanging slightly ajar from his frantic escape.

Sinclair dug through the glove box and the center console for the car until he found a flashlight, then sent the obligatory "Out for food" text to Johnny. Sinclair took a deep breath, tapped the gun against his hip to assure himself that it was still there, and then stepped out onto the overgrown front lawn.

For the third time in as many days, Sinclair sized up the Rochester house, and the house seemed to do the same. They were both old, broken, and in disrepair. And yet despite their outward appearances, both still harbored the capacity to lash out. To take people down with them if the need . . . or the want . . . presented itself.

Sinclair made his way up the steps to the front porch carefully, wincing each time a board screeched, swinging his flashlight around and scanning the tree lines for the mannequins which had disappeared. No. That couldn't be right. The mannequins which Sinclair had mis-clocked earlier. The ones which he thought were situated at 5:00 to the southeast of the house, but which must have been closer to 4:50, or 4:40, where the beam of his light just barely couldn't reach. Sin's earlier read on them must have been just a little bit off. Because why would they have been moved?

Sinclair slid sideways into the house, trying to scan the inside of the house while simultaneously not taking his eyes off the tree line. Things shifted on the edge of his vision. Maybe just a trick of the light. Maybe his wife's ghost again. Sinclair turned, faced the house, and behind him the screen door slapped shut, making Sinclair leap halfway out of his shoes. His gun pressed against his hip, and yet still, despite everything, Sinclair didn't reach for it.

Why bother shooting at shadows? It wasn't the darkness that Sinclair was afraid of. It was all the things hidden in the shadows. The shadows of this house. The shadows of secrets, unspoken knowledge which could have helped Sinclair understand what was really going on. No. A bullet would do nothing against those shadows. But his flashlight might. What secrets could this little beam of light reveal?

The house was empty.

Totally, completely empty. No ghosts flitted about. No person whispered to themselves upstairs. No puppets spun up the turn table in the living room. No puppets were visible anywhere, to Sinclair's left or his right.

He spun in a little circle, panic swelling up in his chest.

Where the fuck were they?

Three days ago, this place had been filled to the brim with the plastic-fleshed, glassy-eyed little bastards. Now, their vacancy set Sinclair more on edge than their creepy presence ever had. There was no way somebody had come in here, cleaned the place out like this while he was away. There were too many dolls. There was too little purpose.

"What the fuck?" he whispered, heading towards the steps upstairs. "What the fuck, what the fuck, what the fuck?"

He thought he could smell the flayed sheep downstairs, starting to rot after days left unattended as he witnessed another rush of movement, upstairs, just outside the field of his vision.

Sinclair swallowed his fear.

It was just his dead wife. Just her ghost. And ghosts couldn't touch you, couldn't hurt you. Especially not Claire. Not wonderful, sweet Claire.

Palms coated with sweat, hands trembling, Sinclair made his way to the top landing, turned towards the last two rooms which he hadn't checked. One on the right side of the hall, one at the end. He moved forward slowly, weight on his toes, ears trained to pick up any sound, no matter how slight.

He gripped the knob to the door on his right, exhaled slowly, and swung the door open, praying he wouldn't come face to face with his decaying wife.

He found nothing more than a linen closet, three sets of sheets folded poorly and stuffed onto the shelves.

Sinclair groaned and closed the door. He swept his flashlight across the landing to make sure he was still alone and found nothing more sinister than a thousand dust motes drifting about, watching over his shoulders.

"It's just a house. It's empty. You're making a fool of yourself, then you'll go back to the station and you'll get some food on the way, and Johnny will call you names and crack a joke about "fast food" not being so fast.

"Just one more room. Just one more room," he whispered the words, filling the unnerving silence with his own voice to help break some of the tension in the air as he gripped the second knob, turned it, and shoved, the door sticking slightly in its frame, swollen from the heat.

When this door popped open, there was so much more than just a simple linen closet to find.

The bedroom was in a state of manic disrepair, the mattress flipped up vertically against a wall, newspapers scattered all over the place. Pages and pages of loose leaf paper had been stapled to the wall to Sinclair's left as whatever Rochester was working on had taken over all available floor space and begun creeping its way towards the ceiling like vines.

Sinclair patted his pockets, looking for his phone. Shit. Had he left it in the car? He needed to take pictures of this and . . . damn it. He'd left it in the car after sending Johnny that text.

Sinclair dropped to his knees, careful not to disturb any of the evidence in the room, but drawing his flashlight and his eyes closer so that he could make out what Rochester had been mapping out.

He saw articles about Meth. Diagrams and instructions about how to make and produce meth. The process for what chemicals to mix, where, and how.

Had Rochester been making meth? The dude seemed out of his mind on *something*, but Sinclair hadn't pegged him as a drug addict for some reason. He just didn't seem the type. And if he was an addict, wouldn't he be going through withdrawals in his cell by now? Maybe that's what the self-mutilation had been about the other day. But no, that didn't quite add up.

More fucking puzzle pieces that didn't fit together.

Sinclair was about to stand up when a piece of paper, no, a picture, closer to the center of the room, caught his eye.

Protocol be damned, Sinclair swept a couple of pages about the methamphetamine creation process out of the way and slid forward. It was a picture of the Gattis Lumber Mill. Rochester had circled the smoke stacks above the mill with a red marker and written 'Exhaust' beside them in big, bold, blocky letters.

Now THAT made sense.

Gattis seemed 100% like the type of creep who would be into drug production. A lumber mill would be a decent front for some sort of a large scale operation. A couple of pieces clicked into place for Sinclair.

So Gattis was into drug manufacturing. Or at least, that's what Rochester believed. And if that's what Rochester believed, then could that be a motive for . . . whatever was happening here? Gattis ran a drug operation, the mayor was in on it, Rochester and . . . somebody else, had to be . . . decided to whip out some frontier justice on their asses.

It still didn't explain the dead lambs in the basement. And without knowing who Rochester was working with, there was no way to know how Rochester was coordinating everything from inside his jail cell. There were still big chunks missing from this picture, but damn it, Sinclair felt like he finally had the puzzle's outline put together. Just had to fill in the middle now.

Why was Rochester so fired up about the drug distribution?

Who else was involved?

Sinclair thought about the kid, Barker, again, but no, the fear in his eyes had been too real that first day when Johnny picked him up. The kid wasn't in on whatever this was, he'd just stumbled into it, exposed it.

Sinclair stood and sent his light's beam on a quick pass around the other papers on the floor. More and more details about the ins and outs of meth production. Background research about the Gattis family and their business, with a hundred pictures of Ethan Gattis smiling back at Sinclair.

He'd need to be the next person Sinclair visited. He wondered how fast Johnny could get a warrant for–

God damn it. Johnny.

This is why Johnny had been so cagey recently, wasn't it? The reason he had been so hesitant to investigate anything about the mayor. Why he had gotten so frustrated when they questioned Gattis at the mill. How much was he in on this? If Gattis was making enough money from a meth production ring, could he have bought off the Mayor? Could he have paid off Johnny?

Sinclair couldn't tell his friend about this. Not until he knew how deep Johnny was into it. But he needed to get back to the station now. He needed to confront Johnny, at last, about why he wasn't shooting straight with Sinclair. Then they would either go to the Gattis Mill together to make the arrest, or Sinclair would throw Johnny into the slammer right alongside Rochester while he sorted things out for himself.

This wasn't the way Hollow Hills was supposed to go.

Some fresh fucking start, he thought as he turned to leave the room.

His wife stood at the top of the stairs now, red blistered skin outlined by her blond hair scorched black. Remnants of her favorite black t-shirt and jeans still clung to portions of her flesh.

Sinclair screamed, unable to help himself, and fell backwards scattering Rochester's notes all across the bedroom floor. He landed, hard on his hip, but never took his eyes off his wife, who turned and pointed at the door to Rochester's room. The one where he'd found the crazy man that first day, lying naked in his bed, surrounded by his dolls.

Claire stared back at him, as much as she could 'stare' with her right eye boiled and popped, her left one cloudy and unseeing.

"What are you doing here?" Sinclair screamed. "Why didn't you just stay in Charlotte? Why are you following me? I can't do this anymore, Claire. I can't. I can't. I can't," he shouted words at the ghost, but she stood stoic, unwavering, as Sinclair fought to maintain his sanity.

Claire thrust her finger, a second time, towards the door, and was it just Sinclair's imagination, or was there a second lady in the hall now too? One directly behind Claire, trying to match her movements exactly, but just a little bit off. Just a little bit slower with the finger thrust?

Just what he needed. Something else to be confused about.

Sinclair rose to his feet, found his flashlight again, and approached his dead wife slowly, reminding himself of his mantra from earlier.

"It's Claire. She wouldn't hurt you. It's Claire. She wouldn't hurt you."

As he approached, Claire floated around sideways, simultaneously barring Sinclair's path to the steps and giving him an opening to reach Rochester's door.

"Oh, thanks," he said, a bit sarcastically, trying to combat his stomach-churning terror with a clip of humor. It worked. A bit. It felt like he was joking around with Claire again from the before-times and that familiarity helped his hand stop shaking like a damn chihuahua, helped him grip Rochester's door handle with a little bit of confidence.

"Not gonna find another naked dude in here this time, I hope," he doubled down on the jokes. But still, Claire's expression didn't change. Could she hear him? Would her expression change even if she did? Sinclair considered pouring his heart out. Telling his dead wife how much he missed her. How much he wanted her back. But he must have hesitated too long at the door frame because Claire thrust her finger at the door again, causing her image to judder, splitting in two for a second time. This time Sinclair saw a second face behind his wife's. Another woman, this one with jet black hair, her arms wrapped around Claire as if she was holding her up.

"The fuck is going on?"

The door flew open in Sinclair's hands, and Claire's ghost vanished.

Sinclair stayed there, rooted to the spot, for the next minute, looking from the suddenly vacant front steps, into the eerie, dark bedroom to his left. The one which his wife had wanted him to revisit for some reason.

He blinked. Gripped the flashlight a thousand times tighter than he needed to. Screamed again.

"The FUCK is going on?"

# THE ROOM

**WHY HAD CLAIRE** railroaded him into Rochester's bedroom?

A bloody angel lay, caked to Rochester's sheets from where the man had laid in the gore before, the bed itself and the furniture untouched since that day. Just now all the dolls, toys, and puppets were vacant.

Weight on his toes, flashlight branded like a weapon, Sinclair crept to the wardrobe nearby, peeking behind it as if all of the dolls might have fallen behind there somehow. But no, the beam of his light revealed nothing but a family of dust bunnies.

Sinclair turned back to the rest of the room and screamed. He stumbled backwards, yet again, at the sight of his dead wife. She had entered the room without a whisper, and now her unstable image quaked, floating on top of the bed, her feet positioned right in the center of Rochester's crimson stain. Had she glid through the room while Sinclair's back was turned, or just teleported to the spot? Who the hell knew. Ghost physics were the worst.

"What's over there, babe? What do you want me to see?"

Claire's ghost kept her head down, hair hanging across her face, but she pointed her finger, flickering into and out of existence, down towards at the bed. But there was nothing there except the bed sheets and the blood stains. So what?

Maybe she wasn't pointing towards the bed.

What about through the bed? Under the bed?

Sinclair dropped to one knee, letting his eyes flit away from Claire for a fraction of a second as he checked the dark crawl space behind Rochester's drooping sheets. He crawled up to the bed and reached out with trembling fingers to grab the sheet's frayed edge. He took one more deep breath to steady his nerves, then pulled back the white curtain to reveal . . . nothing.

The space below the bed was completely vacant.

No shoes were discarded underneath, no boxes had been hidden under there for storage, no nothing. Just another couple of dust bunnies and some splinters jutting up from the old boards.

Confused, Sinclair dropped the bed sheet and looked back up towards his wife. But Claire was gone. Instead, Sinclair found himself staring straight into the face of a woman who he'd never seen before. A woman who looked as dead as the grave.

This specter looked worse for wear than Claire.

Whereas Sinclair had grown used to the white, empty stare of his dead wife, this woman's eyes were pitch black and filled with hate. When she screamed, her spittle and rancid, dead breath slapped Sinclair in the face like a hot oven just being opened. She lunged forward at Sinclair, grabbing him by the sides of his head and digging her thumbs into his temples. Dueling sensations of burning and freezing bored through Sinclair's consciousness, blinding him. He felt the ghost woman's fingers slide past his skin, past his bone, into his brain itself, and as the real world slipped away, Sinclair felt his body fall down, down, down . . .

# THE DREAM

**SINCLAIR'S EYES OPENED**, but he knew they weren't his own eyes. His wrists burned and he could feel ropes digging into his flesh even though he knew that this wasn't his own skin, those weren't his own wrists. In a strange, dream-like logic, Sinclair knew without really knowing, that he had woken up in the body of the ghost woman from Rochester's bedroom.

His vision came back to him slowly, and Sinclair looked down to find arms that were too pale to be his, long fingers which were too slender with nails that were too long, a wedding ring that was gold instead of silver, with a plain ovular diamond set on his ring finger.

What was happening?

His hearing came back to him. At first the voice of the man was muffled, like Sinclair was listening to him speak from underwater, but the words slowly started to gain clarity. He recognized the speaker.

"Ye thought ye could screw with our operation, huh? Thought you could stop the Gattis family from conducting our business? Well, I've got news for ye, sweet-stuff. The Gattis Family was here long before you started your meddling. We'll be here long after you're done. Yep. Looong after."

Gattis chuckled as if he was telling a joke and he walked into view.

But despite his distinctive drawl, it took Sinclair a minute to recognize Gattis standing in front of him. He was younger now. So young. Instead of a head of grey, balding hair, Gattis now had a big, blonde bob. Was that a wig? No. Because his skin was different too. No longer wrinkly and beaten down with age. Gattis was suddenly younger. Stronger. Healthier.

Sinclair looked down at the ropes binding his- not his- wrists again.

"Oh, Mrs. Rochester. Beatrice. Our family's been doing this for years. Years and years. And you think that just because you're some kind of a freak with a kinky little book, you'll be able to stop what we're doing? Honey. I know you and your husband ain't from around here, but let me explain how this all works. The mill makes the money. The townsfolk need the money. The townsfolk need us. So whatever you were trying to do with all them voodoo dolls and such in the woods? That shit needs to stop."

Gattis paused here, turned towards Sinclair, Beatrice, whoever he was, to make sure he was still paying attention.

"Now I don't much believe in your witchy ways. Ain't never had room in my heart for no magic 'cept the magic of Jesus." He pronounced the name Jay-sus.

"But there's some other people around here who are a bit more paranoid I guess. People who are gonna blame all their little accidents on the weirdo in the woods who just can't keep to herself."

"Oh, Mr. Gattis" he said, in some mocking voice. "I couldn't make my shipment today 'cause my hands went numb while I was working. I think it was the witch."

"Oh, Mr. Gattis. I'm thinking she cursed this batch of product. I don't trust it enough to pick it up myself, could you help me?"

"Things like that," he sounded normal again. "So, you understand my predicament, don't you? Even if all your spells and dolls and such are nonsense, as I'm convinced they are, you're having an impact on my bottom line. Giving all my lazy, undedicated workers a brand new excuse to use. And I just can't have that. So I've gotta find some way to cut out the lies. Stop the bleeding, so to speak."

He chuckled at that.

"Awkward what has to happen next, huh?"

He nodded to somebody on Sinclair's left and Sinclair felt his head turn. Three men stood there, two of them familiar to Sinclair. Barker Davis's dad stood in front, a baseball bat brandished in his hands. Behind him, Mayor Bellman held a hand in front of his face, studying his palm as closely as possible, maybe ashamed of what he was bearing witness to, maybe anticipating what was about to happen. Not wanting to watch. And then third stood a man who Sinclair didn't recognize. A man wearing a Sheriff's uniform. Johnny's predecessor.

Mr. Davis stepped forward and adjusted his grip on his bat.

"Gentlemen, remember what's at stake here today. Remember why this is necessary. This woman was going to tear down our very way of life. And what's one person's sacrifice for the betterment of our community.

The Sheriff backed up towards the door, and Sinclair felt a pang of hope that maybe he was going to get help. Maybe he was going to do his duty, put a stop to this whole scene.

But instead he just checked the lock. Made sure it was fastened shut.

The first swing of Mikey Davis's bat was too low. Sinclair felt his jaw crack in half, but it wasn't a kill shot. His vision erupted in a thousand fireworks, and the pain was incredible, but Beatrice . . . Sinclair . . . Beatrice was still conscious when gunshot ripped through the door.

She, he, they heard Gregory Rochester's voice screaming something about his wife as Mayor Bellman shouted something about the Sheriff being hit. It was hard to tell exactly what was being said. Words lost their meaning behind the fire of a broken jaw.

Sinclair's eyes drifted upwards just in time to see Mikey Davis, distracted by the gunshot near the door, but still rearing back to deliver his second blow.

"Take Gregory alive! I want to make him watch," Gattis said, his voice still cool and calm despite the chaos of the moment.

Mikey stalled his swing, looking to Gattis, then back towards the commotion at the door. There were another pair of gunshots. Beatrice. Sinclair. Beatrice slumped to their right in the chair, too weak to stay up straight anymore.

"There we are," Gattis said. "There we are. Mr. Davis, go ahead. Then Gregory? You and I are gonna have a little talk."

"No!" Gregory Rochester screamed.

And then Mikey Davis took a swing that would have put Babe Ruth to shame, and the lights went out for Beatrice and Sinclair.

# LAST EXIT

SINCLAIR GASPED, his sense of self returned with the second blow of the bat. He recoiled and swung his light up towards the devilish woman on the bed.

But she was gone and his flashlight cut through empty air as if the dead woman, Beatrice, had never existed.

But she had.

Her grey, dead flesh had been right there, gripping his skull like a vice. She hadn't just been some ghostly apparition like Claire. No, Beatrice had a physical form. That's who she was, wasn't it? Rochester's dead wife could grab Sinclair. Hold his head. She could make him see things that weren't really there and she could hurt him.

Two dirty handprints still soiled the bedsheet where Beatrice had gripped the sides of the mattress as she screamed before projecting . . . God. What had that been? Was that her memory? Had Sinclair just experienced Beatrice Rochester's death?

Sinclair had had enough of this house.

He jumped to his feet, legs wobbly and unstable under him as he turned and scrambled out of the room, down the stairs, and back out the front door.

Fuck this house.

Fuck this entire town.

Whatever was happening here, it was more than Sinclair had signed up for.

He slammed the door to Johnny's truck closed, flicked on the overhead light, and immediately checked the back seat. No more ghosts were going to get the jump on him, damn it.

The back seat was empty, but Sinclair raised his eyes and saw the outlines of two women, illuminated by the moonlight, watching him from the upstairs windows.

Claire.

Beatrice.

Were they friends? Could ghosts be friends? What was happening?

"Stay! There!" Sinclair shouted, slamming his fist against the dashboard in a frustrated, desperate attempt to feel like he had some control again.

He looked back up to the window, where the women had vanished, then hightailed it away from the Rochester manor before he could figure out where they had gone. He would never come back to the house again, he resolved. There was too much evil energy in the air here. Too many mysteries drawing out the worst of his paranoia. Too much dark energy buoying Claire's spirit up to the surface. And that other woman . . . the one who Sinclair felt certain he had seen before. Not decaying and dead like that, but still.

The truck rumbled back towards town, and for a few blissful final moments, Sinclair was so lost in his own thoughts about Johnny, meth, vanishing dolls and appearing dead women that he didn't notice the red glow of the fire which had taken over the town in his absence.

# LET IT BURN

**THERE WAS NO** way to describe the scene besides "bedlam." Sinclair whipped his truck back onto Main Street and slammed on his brakes, the truck skidding to a halt, leaving Sinclair staring down the road with his jaw on the floor. Flames had engulfed two of the buildings already, the liquor store and the botanist's nursery if Sinclair's mental map was right, but the flames were so high that there were few distinguishing features left to the building. Beside the used-to-be liquor store, Mama Jean's restaurant had started to catch on as well, and even if a fire truck had shown up right then and right there, the building was doomed. It had been built too close to the liquor store, with the alley that separated them narrow enough for the fire to stretch across. The boards that made up Mama Jeans were too old, too neglected, to resist the temptation to burn.

Sinclair swung his head around, looking for a fire truck, or maybe some good Samaritans with buckets of water, or anybody with an interest in helping. But the rest of the world seemed more interested in their own self-preservation at the moment. Racing through the shadows around him, Sinclair became aware of all of the people screaming. He killed the truck's engine, opened the door, and got hit with a wave of sound as people's shrieks, cries, and utter terror became suddenly discernable.

Holy shit.

A lady who Sinclair vaguely remembered seeing at the bar that first night came streaking out from behind an elm tree with- was that one of the mannequins?- right on her tail. The tall, pale figure lashed out with a length of marionette strings, lassoing the terrified ladies' right arm to her side and her sandal caught on the lip of the street's curb. She tumbled head over heels across the asphalt. Her shoulder popped, bulging against her skin, free from its socket as the enormous mannequin landed on her. The doll set to work, dropping its elbows forward bent to a point, and it slammed the plastic corners of its elbows into the side of the lady's head, right through her temple.

Sinclair heard the breaks, like a bag of ice being smashed apart, where he stood ten feet away. The side of the lady's face crumpled inwards. Blood burst from her nose and eye holes in a quick, short spurt.

Before he even had a conscious thought about it, Sinclair's gun was in his hands, his finger pulling the trigger, and for the first time in a long, long time, the town's screams were hidden behind the sound of Sinclair's firearm being discharged.

*CRACK*

A hole opened in the puppet's cheek, a chunk of plastic popping off and spinning away. To his left, one of the mannequins from Rochester's house emerged, stalking forward, moving on its own, animated by some unknowable magic.

*CRACK. POP. CRACK.*

Three more shots. Three more holes. The mannequin approached as if nothing was happening. The doll rose from its kill, tried to approach Sinclair, but was snared by its puppet strings, still wound around the dead woman's arm. It sat down and began to untangle itself, head still on a swivel, watching Sinclair with its glass eyes, both seeing and unseeing all at once.

Sinclair couldn't grasp the impossibility of the whole situation. There was too much to process at once. He just kept squeezing his trigger, aiming at the mannequin, then the doll, then the mannequin again, neither of which seemed phased by the bullets punching holes in their figures.

There was a mannequin walking towards him. There was a puppet killing people. Maybe they were animatronics. Maybe somebody somewhere was watching this whole scene, controlling the thing's movements via remote control. Or maybe there were strings hidden where Sinclair couldn't see him. Maybe this was just a massive, elaborate puppet approaching him.

But even as he desperately tried on each pseudo-rational explanation for what he was seeing, Sinclair knew they were full of shit.

His mind's eye was filled with that page from the book.

The page with the voodoo doll.

Dark magic. That's what he was dealing with here.

He didn't know how, or why, but some deep, religious part of Sinclair's being understood perfectly well what was at play here. He just had to make the rest of his rational mind accept it.

CRACK.

The gun was doing nothing.

There was a second flurry of movement to Sinclair's right, charging towards him out of the darkness and Sinclair turned, leveled his gun, and froze just short of pulling the trigger.

Three peacocks came screaming past him, filling the air with their odd velociraptorian shrieks. A small porcelain doll rode on one of the peacock's backs, raising a kitchen knife into the air and stabbing it back down into the black, blue, and increasingly crimson plumage below.

Alongside the avian murder, a child ran, eyes as wide and as white as the moon, dodging beaks, talons, and cutlery in equal measure.

Barker Davis.

His eyes locked on Sinclair, he saw the mannequin approaching, and he spun on his heel, trying to get away from the deepening well of chaos which was engulfing him.

"Run like hell, Mister. Them dolls are gonna kill us."

Sinclair glanced at his gun, glanced at the kid, and dropped the useless weapon. He ran, matching the kid's pace easily and scooping him up, pulling him free from the birds who were toppling sideways, claws raking through the air around Sinclair's ankles.

He ran, the little kid tucked under his arm like a football, away from the mannequin which was still approaching, slowly, but steadily, like the killers in those old '80s horror movies always tended to do. He would catch Sinclair eventually. No need to hurry.

But Sinclair flew like the devil was gaining ground on him, down Main Street towards the flames which had now taken a liking to the Sheriff's Station. Kicking up chunks of asphalt, a kid crying in his arms, Sinclair ran for all he was worth deeper into the heart of whatever-the-hell was going on.

# RED DUSK RISING

IT WAS NAUSEATING, just how much the scene in Hollow Hills echoed the scene from Charlotte from months prior. More than anything, the smell brought Sinclair back.

A burning building doesn't smell the way you'd expect.

The wood smell is there, sure. That scent that the layman associates with bonfires and smoking meats on purpose to set on the dinner table. That could even be described as the predominant smell, sure. But it's the little things that really set a person's mind spinning out of control.

The electrical lines sizzling and popping add a 'pop' to the atmosphere. The shingles and the tar on the roof remember what it was like to be liquid, to be laid down on a roof in the first place, and the sulfur smell they produce harkens back to their origins. There's a sense of turmoil in the air as every knick-knack and doo dad from within the building catches blaze, tries to add their own ten cents to the ceremonies, and it all melds together into something entirely unique. Some scent that violates our concept of what a smell can, or should, be. Like twenty bright, vibrant colors being poured into a cup and mixed together to make black.

Sinclair stood outside the station, his kid, no, Barker, clutched in his arms, trying to stay tethered to the present. He couldn't lose himself to a daydream about Charlotte. Not now. Not with Johnny in danger and Rochester inside, trapped, burning to death before he could give Sinclair any answers about what the hell was going on around here.

Somewhere far from Main Street, a shotgun clapped to life, and Sinclair snapped back to attention.

"Stay here," Sinclair said as he set the kid down on the sidewalk.

"Fuck that, mister. Those things catch back up to me I'm goddamn outta here."

It wasn't the time to be correcting a child's vulgarities, so Sinclair just nodded, looked up and down the street. Behind windows there were flashes of skin, of plastic and porcelain as puppets chased the residents of Hollow Hills through their own homes. The shotgun barked again, cutting through the never-ending chorus of screams which reverberated off the bricks and the trees and the lamp posts all up and down town.

So, Sinclair nodded.

"I'll be right back," he said. And he thought he meant it.

Sinclair hustled towards the flaming Sheriff's department.

"Johnny!"

He tested the door with the back of his hand, found it way too hot to grab with his hand, so he reared back, raised his boot, and kicked the shit out of the door.

It wasn't locked, thank God, so the door broke away without too much resistance and Sinclair stumbled into the main expanse of the station, hands raised, painfully aware of his lack of weaponry.

Inside, the flames hadn't really taken root yet. Smoke trails snaked along the ceiling, and the heat was smothering, but Sinclair could still bear it, could still see through it. But there wasn't any telling how long that would last. The fire had conquered the station's roof already. It was only a matter of time before it ate its way through to the interior.

"Johnny!" Sinclair shouted again.

"In here," came the reply, not from Johnny's office, as Sinclair had expected, but from his right, in the holding cell.

Rochester was gone, and in his place, the Sheriff stood, hands pressed against the back side of the glass, head cocked sideways as he coughed and tried to breathe through the fabric of his shirt. Johnny was beaten and bloodied, his face a swollen mess that would have rendered him completely unrecognizable if it wasn't for the blood-soaked uniform that he wore.

"The hell are you doing in there?" Sinclair shouted as he hustled forward, patting his pockets for his keys.

No keys though. They were still in Johnny's truck.

Shit on a brick.

"Rochester. Puppets. I don't fucking know, Sin, what's happening out there?

Sinclair glanced back towards the front of the Station, towards the road outside, and simply shook his head. There was no explaining it. And there was no time to waste trying. The heat in the room was intensifying, growing more and more overbearing with each passing second.

"They threw my keys under O'Hare's desk." Johnny said, pointing across the room as if Sinclair needed some reminder about where O'Hare's desk was located.

Sinclair turned, looked up towards the office and roof which had begun making horrific cracking noises as the fire ate through support beams and rafters. The ceiling and Johnny's office hadn't been totally lost to the smoke yet, and Sinclair thought that if he hurried, maybe he could get Johnny out before he choked to death, or before the roof collapsed in on them.

Without thinking any more about it, Sinclair spun around, bolting for the desk which was stacked with incomplete paperwork and twinkie wrappers. He needed to make the most of every second.

Outside, there was more screaming. A trio of individual voices could be made out now, as some people must have escaped outside. Sinclair worried about Barker. He would have bolted. Was probably gone forever now. Shit, how had he just left a kid in the middle of the road during all this?

"Puppets? Goddamn puppets?" a familiar voice rasped- O'Hare- but Sinclair didn't have time to go check on his fellow officer.

He threw himself to his belly, rolled O'Hare's chair out of the way, and slid a hand under the desk, feeling around for jagged lumps of metal, a key ring. Plastic crinkled as his fingers dug through trash which had accumulated over the years until at last, eureka, something solid.

He grabbed the keys and yanked them back just as the window behind him exploded in a shower of glass, the shotgun he'd heard earlier shattering the front of the Station, sending it cascading down all-around Sinclair in a rain of a thousand shards. The glass reflected the flames as they raced through the air, sending a kaleidoscope of yellows, reds, and oranges dancing across the walls.

Outside, O'Hare stood, half his face missing, replaced with a mask of red and white where the bone showed through. He stood at an awkward angle, vertical until his waist, then keeled to his left like an inflatable balloon man in front of a car dealership with the air leaking out. In his right hand, the shotgun was still pointed at the Sheriff's station, no, at the mannequin which stood between O'Hare and the Sheriff's station.

As Sinclair looked on, a ventriloquist dummy crawled from beneath a nearby car, with both of its legs missing, probably O'Hare's handy work from earlier. It seized the officer's ankle in its tiny hands, opened it's hinged jaw, and clamped down on O'Hare's achilles.

What remained of O'Hare's jaw clenched in pain, but he didn't scream. He just kept his eyes locked on the mannequin and he racked another shell.

"Shannon, run!" Johnny screamed from the containment cell, but it was so pointless. O'Hare was a dead man standing, and even if he wasn't, there was no way O'Hare could hear him. Not over the apocalypse which separated them.

The shotgun exploded again, never mind the fact that O'Hare should have dropped dead 30 seconds prior. Buckshot rocked the mannequin slightly, the wall in front of Sinclair popping like firecrackers, and a sudden sting catching Sinclair's ass. He hadn't been crawling as low as thought he was, apparently.

The shotgun fragment only clipped Sinclair, but it hurt like a mother fucker, and he dropped his hips even lower, continued to crawl towards his chief as the mannequin stepped through the broken glass and entered the Sheriff's Station.

Outside, O'Hare shrieked in pain as two American Girl-esque dolls reached the scene and helped the ventriloquist dummy to relieve the officer of his left foot. The shotgun screamed one final time, but based on the gurgling noises O'Hare started making, the gun failed to save its master. Sinclair lifted his head back up, not looking towards the outside, but he could imagine what the dolls might be doing to the officer.

He bounded towards the door to the holding cell,

"You okay, Johnny?" he asked as he lifted the ring of a thousand keys, the roof overhead crackling and popping in distress.

"I'll be better once we're . . . cough . . . out of here . . . cough."

In the back of the station there was a boom akin to that of the shotgun blast as part of the roof or a wall collapsed at the insistence of the fire. Sinclair's breaths hurt; the dry, super-heated air raking at his lungs whenever he inhaled. There was a surge of heat as the flames consumed the new air, the fresh oxygen, and Sinclair grabbed what he thought was the key to the cell and jammed the sliver of metal into the lock.

It wouldn't fit. Wrong key.

Behind him, shadows shifted about irregularly, and Sinclair glanced to his right just as the mannequin reached him. The oversized doll lunged forward, its hand stabbing through the air where Sinclair's face had been moments before. Sinclair fell backwards, dropping the keys and rolling away from the attack. He popped back up to his feet a few feet farther back from the mannequin whose errant blow had slammed against the glass of the holding cell, causing it to crack in a web-like pattern.

The doll looked back and forth from Johnny to Sinclair, then back to Johnny. It raised its other fist and slammed it down into the glass also, creating a second web of cracks which laced over the first.

Johnny backed up in the cell, moving away from the monstrosity as Sinclair looked back and forth from the mannequin to the keys on the floor, and back to Johnny. Maybe he could jump forward, get the keys, dodge the doll's attack, lure it away, then circle back to undo the lock. But what if he tried the wrong key again? How many times would he be able to try the lock? The mannequin seemed slow, but was it also stupid?

"Hey Sinclair?" Johnny called from the other side of the glass.

Sinclair ignored him though. He needed to think. How to get his friend out . . . ?

He drew a blank as the mannequin punched the glass for a third time, the flames from the station dancing in the fractured reflection.

"Sinclair! Listen to me, damnit!' Johnny shouted, then began to cough and retch from the smoke that entered his lungs.

Sinclair looked, and the expression on Johnny's face overrode any plans Sinclair was trying to make.

Defeat. Sadness. Acceptance.

More dolls, the ones which had killed O'Hare, began to crawl through the broken front window of the Station and another chunk of the roof came tumbling down, engulfed in flames. Sinclair's vision was beginning to swim from the overwhelming heat in the room.

"I'm not leaving you, Johnny."

But even as he said this, the mannequin broke through the glass, the spiderwebs collapsing inwards, giving the nightmare unobstructed access to the Sheriff. There was no way for Sinclair to get around him. There was no way for Johnny to get past. And time had run out. If Sinclair stayed in here any longer he was either going to pass out from the heat or those approaching dolls would rip him apart.

He spared a glance at O'Hare's murderers, saw their plastic faces melting in the heat, but saw them coming at him still, regardless.

What the fuck were these things?

"You've gotta go, Sinclair. I wish I had time to explain . . . cough . . . everything." Johnny's voice was calm, despite the monster climbing into the room with him. He took his time with each word, making sure they were all clear despite his coughing and the rasp which the smoke had introduced to his throat.

"Rochester did this. Rochester did all of this. But he's not . . . wrong . . . cough . . . He's not wrong, Sin. Find him. Stop him. But he's not . . . God damn it. He's not wrong. I'm so sorry I brought you into this, bud. I'm so, so sorry. I thought you could help. I thought we could help each other. But, God damn it. After what happened to his wife? We all deserve this."

At the mention of Rochester's wife, the mannequin froze. The smaller dolls froze. It even seemed like the flames consuming the building froze for a moment.

"Beatrice . . . " Sinclair whispered.

But Johnny would never get to respond. The mannequin reached his prey, finally, and grabbed the left side of Johnny's face with such unchecked force that the thing's thumb gauged straight through Johnny's left eye, its fingers gripping the back of the Sheriff's head with enough force to crack dents into the base of his skull.

Johnny screamed in agony, his voice breaking as the smoke flooded his lungs, and the mannequin lifted him into the air as if he was made of nothing more than styrofoam.

Sinclair ran, taking off towards his right, away from the smaller dolls and hurdling over a piece of smoldering debris from the ceiling, keeping his eyes glued on his friend the entire time. He couldn't force himself to look away.

The mannequin whipped Johnny in the air, his spine flexing backwards and popping at the force of his legs being slung back and forth, and then the mannequin brought the former chief of Hollow Hills' body arcing up, over, around, and down, snapping him in half over the top of the metal bench, still fastened to the floor. The one which Rochester had stood on, hours earlier, imitating the dead Mayor Bellman.

Johnny's skin popped and split over the unyielding metal and his blood gushed forth like a sink being drained, coating the dried blood which Rochester had smeared around hours before.

A new smell joined the symphony of odors in the fire: the heavy, damp smell of life ripped away.

Johnny's eyes were still open, but unseeing as the mannequin raised the Sheriff's corpse high overhead, again. Without any discernible effort, the mannequin was able to rip Sinclair's friend in half like a crab leg, his spine dangling from his top half like a tail.

That was the last Sinclair saw of his friend. The roof over the holding cell finally collapsed and the grotesque scene vanished behind a waterfall of embers, flames, and collapsing architecture.

Sinclair stumbled, his boots toe catching on a fallen chair leg. For a moment he thought it was one of the smaller dolls, so he kicked the chair in a panic, sending it skidding away.

Refocused, he scanned the room, clocked the two slowly advancing marionettes, and he adjusted his course to avoid them as he made his way finally, blessedly, back outside.

# SURVIVOR SONG

**THE FRESH AIR** hit him in the face like being plunged into an ice bath. Sinclair's head spun, his vision blurred, and he nearly fell to his knees as he sucked in deep, clean breaths too fast and succumbed to a coughing fit. The coughing fit devolved into vomiting and smoke-tinged stomach bile raked at his throat, filled his mouth with a flavor that doubled down on his nausea.

But he couldn't stand still. Couldn't stop moving. To be stagnant was to die. That's the lesson he was learning here.

Johnny. Poor Johnny.

After everything the two of them had been through together, everything they were planning to go through together, how had it all been snuffed out so quickly as that?

Sinclair couldn't dwell on that. Not here in the midst of the chaos. He couldn't just slip away under a swell of nostalgia and longing. He tried not to look back at the flaming pile of wood and bricks that used to be the station, and instead Sinclair tucked all thoughts of Johnny away in the same mental lockbox which Claire and Max had been relegated to as he rose to his feet.

Overhead, the smoke from the burning town consolidated like clouds, forming a canopy over the carnage that reflected the shimmering, broken orange light of the wildfire back across the town. Heaven and hell had been inverted, the devil and his minions breaking through the blanket of lava which stretched across the sky, raining down to scorch the earth. As below, so it was above.

Sinclair blinked, rubbed his eyes, and looked around for Barker, even though he knew that the kid was gone. As he should have been. There was no reason for the kid to have just sat there watching O'Hare get torn apart, while the army of the plastic undead massacred everything that had a pulse. Sinclair just had to hope the kid was safe and he had to press on.

But press on to where?

Rochester was the key to all of this, it seemed, but where would the mad man be, if not locked away in the station? Once he escaped, with Johnny locked in the slammer instead, what would Rochester's next move have been?

It was too obvious.

The Toy Store.

Sinclair spat in a desperate effort to relieve the taste of bile from his mouth, and he rose to his feet. His hands were still empty, devoid of anything that resembled a weapon, and he waggled his bare fingers as he looked over his shoulder, back towards the ruined Sheriff's department. The dolls which had been crawling through the station towards him were amorphous by now, their plastic having melted enough to ruin any semblance of arms, legs or faces. All of it dripped and sagged into meaningless heaps atop the Station's cracked white tile floor. The flames consuming the station had tripled in size and intensity since Sinclair escaped and what remained of the dolls weren't moving anymore. Did that mean they were dead? Was dead even the right word for these things?

Re-unanimated.

Maybe that was more accurate.

Sinclair looked towards the rubble where the mannequin and Johnny had been buried. Nothing seemed to be moving in that direction either. So, were those his options for combating these things? Melt them and break them? Bullets sure hadn't seemed to do anything, that was for damned sure.

He rolled his shoulders backwards, tried to stretch a crick out of his neck, and marched towards the Toy Store, still without a plan. Maybe something would come to him as he moved. Or maybe he would just die in the old, run-down shop. It didn't seem to matter much either way. But he couldn't just stand in the middle of the road like an asshole, staring at the rubble where his best friend, his corrupted best friend, lay buried.

He picked his way across and around the broken glass and the bodies which littered the street. O'Hare's corpse wasn't the only one which had dropped while Sinclair was at the station. A man with a blue jean jacket lay sprawled, half on the sidewalk, half on a bush with his elbows snapped, arms bent opposite how they should be. A lady had been suspended from a light post, fishing line, digging into the meat of her arms and her throat like she was a pork loin wrapped by the local butcher who was, it turned out, also dead, split in half in the alley to Sinclair's right.

It was all too much to process. Sinclair tried to turn his mind off, focusing on his steps and keeping his eyes downcast, towards his feet. But the gears in his head wouldn't stop. Couldn't stop.

There were no kids out here. He realized it at first with relief, but then with growing confusion. Why? Kids were always bouncing around the town. Where had they all gone? Surely any kids that were here would have been screaming, crying about the horrors at play. Even if they were exempt from these puppets murderous rampage somehow, where had they all gone?

Were they dead, just somewhere else?

Was this some sort of a Pied Piper scenario? Rochester had always been a toy maker. He must have had a soft spot for kids. But did that mean he would protect them here? Or would they be his targets?

Damn it, this all made so little sense. What did Rochester's wife's death have to do with any of this?

Resurrection.

The word called to him from the book in his bathroom drawer.

Resurrection of Beatrice. But how? Where? If resurrection was real, then where had Beatrice's body ended up? Unless . . .

Images of the dolls all racing about, murdering Hollow Hills residents with a seemingly singular purpose carried Sinclair all the way to the old Toy Shop. How were their actions so in sync? So coordinated?

The answer was right there, but despite everything he'd seen, Sinclair still failed to fully grasp it.

He reached the Toy Store and paused, having to work to catch his breath amid the smoke and the frantic flurry of activity. Somehow the building still stood, free from flames, as if the fire had intentionally burned a path around its sacred halls, the walls of flames keeping their distance from the declared holy ground. And who knew, the way tonight was going. Maybe it had. Maybe the fire had gained sentience also, consuming parts of the town, but not others at the will and urging of Gregory Rochester. Sinclair didn't know the first thing about black magic. Despite how much he had looked at the book, he still had no clue how any of this could or couldn't work. Who was he to assume its limits?

On the ground next to him, a bike lay abandoned. Based on the way weeds had grown up through the spokes, the little fixed-gear had sat there discarded for years. There were no bike thieves in Hollow Hills. There had never been a need for any. Just like Johnny had explained on day one, Hollow Hills was such a nice town. No major crimes. No bike thieves. No mass-genocides of the townsfolk by possessed, blood-lusting puppets.

Surely none of that.

Sinclair reached down and pulled off the bike's rusty chain, removing it from the junk pile with little resistance. The chain was old and heavy, and it jangled when Sinclair waggled it about, instilling him with . . . confidence was too strong of a word . . . but hope, maybe. Courage in the faintest sense against whatever was to come.

He shouldered the entrance to the Toy Store, knocking some of the old boards loose, and crawling inside. He expected to be greeted by dusty shelves. Rows upon rows of googly-eyed, abandoned porcelain figurines, toy trains, and all other reminders of neglected, forsaken childhoods.

He wasn't expecting the unearthed body of Beatrice Rochester.

Her moldy, earth-eaten flesh clung too-tight to her skeleton. Her burial dress and her leathery skin were the only things holding her bones together. Sinclair screamed, fell to his ass, and banged his head against the boards he had just crawled past. His vision swam and the orange light of the room grew darker and darker and darker . . .

# BEATRICE

**LITTLE HANDS GRIPPED** Sinclair's shoulders, and he felt sure this was how he would die. Ripped apart by a goddamn cabbage patch kid. After all the tweakers he had wrestled, the gangsters who had shot at him, and the crooked cops who'd tracked him with their crosshairs, he was going to die at the hands of a possessed Barbie or some shit.

But instead of ending his life, finally sending Sinclair along to the happily ever after, the hands shook him once, twice, then slapped him across the face.

"Wake up, Mister. You can't sleep here."

Barker Davis's voice cut through the darkness and Sinclair reluctantly forced one eye open, found the kid scowling down at him. Behind the Davis kid, the world still shimmered in orange light, the fire still raging outside. So, Sinclair must not have been out for TOO terribly long.

He opened his second eye, allowing the dead woman's body to come back into view over Barker's shoulder. Sinclair's sucked in his breath and Barker tracked his gaze, laughed at him.

"Seriously, mister? She's dead. She's probably the *last* thing we need to be worried about in here."

Barker said this in hushed tones. Even if he wasn't worried about the dead body, he was still on edge. Trying not to draw attention to himself and Sinclair, huddled by the front door. Sinclair noticed now how the boy was crouched, keeping his head down, unmoving and low to the floor.

Smart kid.

Had a mouth on him. And Sinclair would never be able to shake the memory of seeing the child dripping with blood, seated in the front of Johnny's pickup. But he was proving to be more adaptive than Sinclair could have ever guessed. He was still alive in a puppet uprising that had murdered every single officer in the town, which had murdered at least . . . what was it now . . . six adults in front of Sinclair's very eyes and countless more in the shadows, behind closed doors. And still, here was this kid. The only kid Sinclair had even seen since all this kicked off.

If he'd been wearing a hat, Sinclair would have tipped it for him.

Instead, he raised a hand to the kid, trying to get Barker to help him up off the ground. Barker turned though, the request for aid ignored.

Still low, Barker crawled towards an empty shelving unit- the one that the dead body had been arranged atop. Sinclair grunted and sat up, his eyes glued to the corpse.

He recognized her. Not in the sense that he knew her name, or her voice, or anything about her. But he knew that matted black hair, had seen it plastered to the ghost screaming at him from Rochester's bed. He knew the ring which rested on her left hand, had seen it on this same woman's hand when he possessed her body in the dream.

Sinclair rose to his feet, found the bike chain near his hip, and followed Barker, staying low and staying far away from the body on the shelf. She wouldn't get a second chance to leap up and startle the shit out of him.

"It's all about Beatrice," Johnny had shouted as the Sheriff's Station collapsed around him, the mannequin breaking his body.

"But what does that mean?" he whispered to Johnny's memory.

Barker stopped moving now too, pulled his head back from the aisle he had been peeking down and glared at Sinclair.

"Shut up, old man! They'll hear us."

Sinclair waved the kid off. This was important. Apparently. So, Sinclair stood up to his full height, swallowed his nerves, and approached Beatrice Rochester with his crime scene investigator thinking cap on and adjusted. If she dove at him suddenly, then so be it. He needed clues.

The body had been displayed with care, each foot placed intentionally on the ground, arms folded on the dead woman's lap with cushions and pillows scattered across the top of the shelf which held her. Whoever had brought her here, they hadn't just dumped the corpse and left. It was somebody who cared about her, wanted to honor her even in death.

So, Gregory was the logical assumption. If this was his wife.

And it was so obviously, clearly her.

The damage from Mikey Davis's baseball bat was unmistakable. The whole right half of her face was cracked, folded in on itself, and bone shards jutted through the thin, frail remains of her skin at unbelievable angles. But just to make sure . . . yep . . . the same small, generic wedding ring which Sinclair remembered from his out-of-body experience with Beatrice hung loosely on the corpse's decomposing left finger. The light from outside cast plenty of light for Sinclair to slip the band off and find the inscription.

To: Beatrice Rochester. My Love.

Sinclair slipped the ring back on the finger and settled the hand gently back onto the deceased's lap. One hundred percent. No questions asked. This was her.

Barker hissed at Sinclair, throwing his hands up in a 'what are you doing' sort of a manner.

"This is the crazy toymaker's place," the kid growled. "And you know what those things outside are, killing everybody? They're toys! And I'm no great detective like you," he said, the sarcasm dripping from his words, "but methinks there might be a connection there. We need to move. Now stop fondling the dead chick and let's move."

"They killed her. They buried her. Now she's here."

"So fucking what?"

"Why? Why move a body across town to put it in this Toy Shop?"

Maybe they thought they could sell it for a quick buck. Creepy Rochester's Toys 'R' Rot. It doesn't matter anymore. We've got to move."

Sinclair climbed up to the top of the toy shelf.

"Mister what are you . . . "

Now it was Sinclair's turn to silence the kid.

Sinclair crouched beside the corpse, leveling his head with hers, and looked out through the front window of the Toy Store. The windows hadn't been boarded up this high. Or, if they had, somebody would have removed the boards. Beatrice had a clear view of Main Street. Of the hellscape it had become.

"He wanted to let her watch."

Sinclair rubbed a forefinger and a thumb across the bridge of his nose.

"This was all for her."

Outside there was another boom as a gun went off in the distance, but the sounds of people defending themselves were growing more and more distant, more and more infrequent.

Sinclair turned towards Beatrice's hollow, empty eyes.

"You've probably got some pretty decent cursive handwriting too, don't you? Practiced a little witchcraft maybe?"

He was starting to figure it out.

Barker grabbed Sinclair's foot, pulled on it, a wild look in his eyes. He pointed back towards the front door of the toy store where Rochester's second mannequin had suddenly appeared.

# RISE, BARKER DAVIS

**THE ORANGE GLOW** from outside danced along the walls of the toy shop, allowing Sinclair to track the mannequin's progress. The flames' light made the whole room feel alive, as if the walls were quivering with energy, the shadows rollicking in anticipation of the next kill. Strange how so many inanimate things- flame, light, wood, glass, and steel could come together to give the impression of something organic. Something with a mind of its own. And in the midst of this false reflection of life, the mannequin soldiered forward.

Sinclair and Barker lay flat against the floor, crawling in the opposite direction of the mannequin, along an aisle filled with Legos and Erector sets, towards an open door in the back of the shop. Sinclair tried to breathe as softly as possible, but it felt like his heart was beating loud enough to give their position away despite him, stealth be damned.

He peeked behind him and saw the mannequin's shadow splayed across the back wall. It was still hovering near Mrs. Rochester's corpse. Sinclair reached a hand back, placed it on Barker's shoulder, and gently eased him around the corner, into a perpendicular aisle which ran along the back side of the store. The door was only a few feet away. They could get in there, close the door gently behind them, and be free from the mannequin's sight. That was, if the mannequin even had a sense of vision. It had no eyeballs. Just sculpted blobs of plastic. How was it following them? How was it tracking him?

No. This was stupid. There was no applying logic or science to what was happening here. No rational biology to be applied to a mannequin chasing them. He just had to get through the door, barricade his path as well as possible, and keep moving. Gregory was bound to be in here somewhere. It was just a matter of where.

A hissing sound reached Sinclair's ears and Sinclair jumped sideways, pulling his hand away from some rubber snakes in a nearby bin.

He sucked in his breath, barely avoided screaming, but his fear was misplaced. The snakes sat still, the same as they always had.

So, what was making the hissing sound?

Beside him, Barker twitched and yelped, his voice piercing the stillness in the Toy Store like a siren.

Barker's body rose up, up, up off the floor and it took Sinclair too long to recognize the puppets and their strings hanging from the ceiling. Overhead, puppets crawled like spiders across the rafters, tied off their strings over the aisles of toys, and descended slowly, so slowly that Sinclair hadn't noticed them as they reached the boy, grabbed him, and began reeling him back in. They grinned down at Sinclair, the cuts which shaped their mouths all turned up in the corners, wooden and plastic cheeks dimpled with sinister, fake enjoyment.

"Max!" Sinclair realized he had yelled the wrong name.

He gritted his teeth and tried to shut out the realization that he was losing a second child to the embers of a burning building. The echoes of his past rushed across him, the current blinding as he swung the bike chain at one of the puppets that hung near his face. He immediately regretted the attack. The links of metal proved to be a wild, imprecise weapon and the chain arced higher and farther than Sinclair had intended, catching Barker on his foot.

The boy cried out either in pain or in fear as he rose into the air quicker and quicker. 6 feet, 7 feet, 8 feet, out of Sinclair's reach, but Sinclair kept swinging his chain in fury, lashing out at anything that *was* in reach. Rows of toys broke and scattered. Metal shelves howled and bent, and then the mannequin, zeroed-in on the chaos, entered the chain's range. The chain bit at the monster's plastic skin, but it reached a hand towards Sinclair's face unabated. Overhead, Barker's screams were stifled. Some of the puppets had ripped their miniature clothes free and used them to gag the child. Now they were all scuttling across the roof, dragging their kill towards a hole that led to the second story like an army of ants carrying away a dead wasp.

But wait. No. They were splitting into two groups, weren't they? As most of the puppets dragged Barker away, kicking and bucking, but no longer screaming, another collection had made their way towards Beatrice Rochester. They dropped their lines around where she sat and lowered themselves in awkward jerky motions as Sinclair dodged under the mannequin's hand. He landed one more blow on the thing's elbow, and then plowed a path through the scattering of toys towards the door he'd been targeting.

The puppets reached Beatrice. They hoisted her towards the ceiling the same as they had raised Barker.

Up. Up. Up. Whatever was going on here, it was up.

Stairs. He needed stairs.

The mannequin kept pace behind Sinclair as he stumbled forward, abandoning its previous slow stalking and hastening after Sinclair with something that resembled urgency. It didn't want him to reach the door.

Sinclair's foot snagged on a twist of metal. He fell, spinning to his left and trying to avoid lashing himself with the bike chain.

He failed.

The tip of the metal whip split his skin with ease as his shoulder hit the ground. Something crunched, and at first Sinclair thought it was his bones. Maybe some ribs. But the lack of pain caused Sinclair to shift about and he located the wooden helicopter he'd landed on, its blades snapped by the weight of his body.

Sinclair slung the toy at the mannequin and it bounced off the impassive brute's face harmlessly. It was hopeless. There was no stopping this thing. At the station they'd had to drop the entire building on the creature to get it to stop, and even then, Sinclair wasn't sure the first mannequin wasn't just slowly working its way free from the rubble.

What were these things?

How could you kill them?

Overhead, Beatrice's body was shuttled towards the same hole Barker had been dragged through, the puppets carrying her corpse carefully, gently, like a chain of ceiling-bound pallbearers. They kept Beatrice's dead arms pinned to her dead sides and minded her head, supporting her neck as they carefully maneuvered her around the cross-beams and light fixtures.

Something about the way they moved, all working together, as a single hive-mind, made it finally, *finally*, click in Sinclair's head.

All the lambs sacrificed in Gregory Rochester's basement.

The dolls. The fucking dolls everywhere.

The book about resurrection.

Beatrice.

Sinclair propped himself up on his elbow and tried to look into the eyes of the mannequin that now stood directly over him, feet planted on either side of his hip.

"So, you're Beatrice, huh?"

The dolls on the ceiling ceased their scrabbling.

The mannequin froze, hand extended towards Sinclair's throat.

Even outside, the sounds of the chaos seemed to stall as across Hollow Hills, Beatrice's collective consciousness, summoned into the bodies of countless puppets, heard themselves being recognized. Called out for what they were.

"Welcome back, I guess."

The mannequin's hands lurched the rest of the way down to seize Sinclair by the hair. It dragged Sinclair, kicking and screaming, towards the stairs he had been fighting so hard to reach, moments earlier as outside the rest of Beatrice Rochester's hive mind resumed their assault on the citizens of Hollow Hills.

# A PYRE FOR MY LOVE

**THE MANNEQUIN DRAGGED** Sinclair all the way up to the roof access hatch. Three flights of stairs, probably, but Sinclair lost his ability and his willingness to count in his pain. The steps beat his ribs and his hips as he was dragged up them. His head was on fire as the mannequin forced a few hundred hair strands to move 200 lbs. of man. Sinclair grabbed the thing's wrist and pulled himself along to ease some of the tearing, but it still wasn't enough. By the time the mannequin dropped him on the roof, blood was leaking down Sinclair's face from all the places his hair had been torn out.

He lay still on the roof for a few minutes, eyes fluttering open and closed, just trying to recompose himself before Sinclair finally had the ability to sit up and gauge his situation.

All around him, the children of Hollow Hills sat. Some cried. Some just stared at the flames. But each one was accompanied by a toy. Some puppet, doll, or action figure hugged them, sat with them, and tried to provide comfort for them. This nightmare would be over soon, and as horrible as everything was, they were at least not alone. Barker Davis, still bound, had been deposited near the back of the crowd and had mostly ceased his struggling. He stared around at everybody else on the roof with wide eyes and a slack-jawed expression of surprise plastered to his face. Five dolls sat by Barker, either on guard duty or for support, it didn't seem like even they had decided yet.

And in front of it all, Gregory Rochester sat atop a pile of old, weathered wooden pallets. His crazed grin was still plastered to his face, his cuts and lacerations from earlier beginning to scab over, leaving him looking sickly, patched together, and out of his goddamn mind.

Beside Gregory sat the body of his dead wife, her empty eye

sockets gazing out across the sea of children and puppets like a mother watching over her flock. Gregory held one of his wife's rotten hands in his own, and with his other hand he turned the pages of some storybook reading it aloud to everybody in attendance. Sinclair focused, trying to make out the words to the story through the din of crying and sniffling children.

What was he reading? This wasn't the Berenstain Bears. Wasn't some Mother Goose nursery rhyme.

"And even though the wicked people from the town were so, so bad, their children were so, so good. The little ones had never done anything wrong in their lives. They had nothing to atone for.

'I'm glad the evil parents are gone,' said Duck. 'For the world is nicer and safer without them in it.'

'And I'm glad the children are safe,' said Fox. 'For they are the future. A chance to build a better world.'

'And I'm glad the toymaker got his wife back,' said the Sheep. 'For they had a love that was truer and deeper than any other."

Gregory Rochester kept doing different voices for the different animals as he read, and Sinclair swallowed the lump in his throat. Holy shit, Sinclair had never grasped just how deranged the toymaker really was. Seeing him covered in his own blood was one thing. Any tweaker on a bad trip could have devolved into that. But this was completely, utterly unhinged.

Sinclair tried to stand, but the mannequin beside him clamped a hand on his shoulder, holding him in place.

"And what of the other police officer, asked the Bear," Gregory 'read' in a low, grumbling voice. "The one who didn't know what he had walked into? The one who didn't know how evil the town really was? How they'd killed the toymaker's wife when she tried to stand up for what was right? What will happen to him?"

All of the doll's heads creaked around simultaneously, turning their glassy eyes and porcelain faces to focus on Sinclair. He sat uncomfortably, the mannequin's fingers digging into his bones.

"Ah. He's a special case." Gregory didn't look up at Sinclair, though he was clearly aware of his presence, and was speaking indirectly to him, through him.

"You see, his wife spoke to Mrs. Beatrice. And his wife told Mrs. Beatrice so many stories about their love. His innocence. How he was a good man that would do the right thing, once he saw the depths of the town's depravity."

Sinclair wanted to scream. What the fuck did he mean, Beatrice had spoken to Claire? If there was any truth to that, any at all, then Claire really was still out there . . . somewhere. It would mean the ghosts he'd been seeing weren't just his own neurosis. And if she was real, then he could bring her back. He would find any way, any means . . . .

He stopped. He saw himself reflected in Gregory Rochester. Recognized the beginnings of the toy maker's madness etched in his own story and knew that if he followed this line of thinking any further, even a single thought further, then the cracks in his understanding of good, evil, life, death, madness, and sanity, would shatter forever.

He stopped it.

In that moment, Sinclair finally steeled himself by accepting the truth he'd been fighting since Charlotte. He came to the realization that he'd literally been running away from for months.

Claire was gone.

Max was gone.

There was no avoiding it. No forgetting it. No way he could-no- no way he *should* try to bring them back.

And if he tried? If he went down the same road that Gregory Rochester had, then he would just end up here. The wake of obsession had the power to destroy, not just his life, but the lives of everyone he surrounded himself with. Johnny was dead. All of these kids' parents? Presumably dead.

And for what?

So Gregory Rochester could hug some animated plastic facsimile of Beatrice again?

Sinclair slumped down and the mannequin let him. He dropped to the roof of the Toy Store, face buried into his hands, trying to hide his tears from the hundreds of dolls, puppets, and mannequins that had their eyes fixed on him.

Fixed.

How could he fix this?

He wished he still had his gun; thought about it lying on the street down below, surrounded by chunks of plastic and cotton fluff from the dolls he'd shot. The ones which hadn't been phased by his bullets.

But Gregory would be phased.

If only Sinclair had held on to his gun, like Johnny told him to do on that first day, he could end this shit right now.

If only.

"So that's it, then." Gregory Rochester said from his throne of pallets. "I give you a chance to fill the hole in your heart and you reject it?" Gregory said, abandoning the guise of reading a story now. He looked up and put his attention squarely on Sinclair's broken, sobbing form.

When Rochester tried to stand, the toll that this whole endeavor had taken on him became obvious. His skin split, reopening in the places where he had clawed himself open to mirror the bloody Mayor Bellman. His back was bent and his eyes glittered with pain as his blood leaked from the reopened wounds.

Around him, puppets leapt to help, climbing on top of each other, forming miniature towers to support their master, their husband, in his quest to stand up straight.

One bullet. That's all Sinclair needed. One fucking bullet.

As if it could sense his thoughts, the mannequin swung its free hand around and punched Sinclair in the gut, knocking the wind from him. Dribbles of spit burst from Sinclair's lips and his vision went white for a second as he gasped for breath.

How could he stop this? Gregory's obsession had spawned more monsters than Sinclair could ever hope to stop on his own.

But he wasn't alone, was he? Sinclair glanced up, ever so slightly turning his eyes to the right where the dolls that had been holding Barker Davis back were gone, hurrying to help Gregory rise to his feet.

In their absence, Barker Davis had risen, unimpeded, disregarded, and Sinclair smiled as the boy reached into his pocket for . . . the whistle.

He blew the whistle with enough force to make the veins in his temples bulge, but Sinclair could hear nothing. The other children on the roof didn't seem like they could hear anything. And, most importantly, Gregory Rochester didn't seem like he could hear anything. The roof seemed silent, save for the roar of the flames below, the sniffles of the newly dubbed orphans, and eventually, softly, in the distance, the beating of wings.

The first peacock burst through the flames behind Gregory Rochester like a phoenix, the tips of its grand feathers leaving smoke trails like a plane practicing cloud writing. Its talons were out, its beak was open, and the prehistoric scream which emanated from the peacock triggered every primal instinct in Sinclair to run, to hide.

The raptors were here.

More beating wings could be heard as a second, third, and fourth peacock managed to flap their ways over the edges of the building, fighting gravity and instincts of self-preservation to respond to their child's summons.

The mannequins, dolls, and puppets froze. Gregory Rochester threw himself back down to the floor, narrowly dodging the sharp beak of the phoenix peacock from behind him.

For the first time, Sinclair saw a new emotion glean past the madness in the toymaker's eyes.

Fear.

Confusion.

Finally, here was something the mad man hadn't accounted for.

There was a single moment where the whole rooftop seemed to hold its collective breath, and then the war ensued.

Maybe the peacocks mistook the buttons on the dolls' clothes for food. Maybe they recognized the danger their boy was in and were acting to protect him. Sinclair would never know. But backed by a wall of flames, Barker Davis's peacock army leapt to the air, wings flapping, feathers splayed, vocal chords straining as they launched their assault on everything and anything they saw on the roof.

The mannequin released its grip on Sinclair and rose back to its full height, lumbering forward to protect Gregory and leaving Sinclair free to run for his own life. Children screamed and leapt to their feet, suddenly knocked from their trance and looking for a way to escape. Within moments, two of the birds bore down on Sinclair, screeching violently, and Sinclair threw up his hands, his thin fingers trying in vain to protect his face.

Fortunately, the birds only got one peck in before Barker reached the scene.

"Not him, you dumbasses. The other one! The other one!" Barker yelled as he charged forward.

The peacocks rose back up, one's beak dripping blood from where it had stabbed Sinclair's hand. Jesus, it had really been about to take one of his eyes, hadn't it? What the shit was wrong with these birds?

Barker blew into his whistle again and the peacocks turned to face their little master. Barker turned towards the rest of the warzone and the birds and Sinclair all followed his gaze into the tempest of arms, legs, and claws.

The screaming kids bumped into each other as they hurriedly dropped the dolls which they had been holding, each realizing in a wave of loss and sadness, that they were alone now. That their parents were gone, and that the world was on fire.

None of them handled the realization well.

Who would have expected them to?

Barker Davis's brothers ran up to him, from the masses, and grabbed his hands.

"Go," Sinclair said to the three of them. "Get everybody else downstairs. Take Main Street back to the woods, away from the fires. It's just the town burning for some reason. Get free of the town and get to safety. I'll take care of this."

For the first time ever, Barker didn't argue. He just narrowed his eyes, scowled, and shouted "This way, snot-heads!" towards the others. He waved an arm as if to summon the orphans to him and, thankful to have somebody that seemed like an authority figure taking charge, the rest of the kids all followed.

"Help my birds!" Barker yelled at Sinclair. The child tossed Sinclair his whistle, then raced off, ushering the little ones back down the stairs.

Sinclair caught the toy and nodded, stupidly. How the hell he could help the birds, he had no clue. They seemed to be doing just fine on their own.

He looked on in awe-struck horror as a ventriloquist dummy was ripped in two. Another peacock had shoved its head so deep into one doll's stuffing that its beak had actually broken through the opposite side, was shoving through the stitching like a Xenomorph being hatched. And on the opposite end of the chaos, Gregory Rochester clung to his wife's body like a life preserver.

The largest of the peacocks had honed in on him and was side-stepping to try to get a good angle on the toy maker, bristling and preparing to make its charge.

Gregory was weeping, yelling at the birds to stop hurting his beloved Beatrice.

"You're hurting her! You're hurting her all over again. This damned town. Why can't this damned town just leave us alone!"

Maybe that was it. The peacocks knew what to attack. Or, more specifically, who to attack. If Sinclair could kill Beatrice for good, maybe that would put a stop to this whole circus. If this was all an attempt to resurrect her, then maybe taking her out would end it all. Like ripping the battery from a malfunctioning toy.

It was worth a shot.

There was a 2x4 on the roof nearby, so Sinclair, using the peacock's attack as a distraction, hustled over to it, moving low, slow, and steady, trying not to draw attention to himself. But Gregory, and the puppets it seemed, had lost their interest in Sinclair.

A peacock screamed as one of the porcelain dolls reached the bird's eyes and started swatting at the bird's face, digging around to find the soft, vulnerable parts of its iris.

Another peacock dove at this puppet, trying to save its friend, but it was too late. The doll's arm plunged, elbow-deep into the bird's skull and the creature fell sideways, its wings flapping their last flaps as it tumbled over the side of the roof. There was a burst of flames as the bird hit something on fire in the alley below.

Perfect.

Not for the bird. It was sad that the bird was dead. But something was on fire down below. Sinclair could use that.

He didn't give himself a chance to think. Instead, Sinclair raised the 2x4 over his shoulder, he lowered his head, and he charged into the fray, making a beeline straight for Beatrice Rochester's corpse.

Beaks clipped him.

Puppets scratched at him, trying to take out his legs.

But Sinclair muscled his way through them all. He was bigger than these things. They were all meaner than he was, but damnit, he wasn't about to get bullied off a roof by a goddamn Cabbage Patch Kid.

Pain engulfed his right leg as one of the dolls hacked at his shin with something sharp. Was that a saw? Where did the puppets find a saw?

It didn't matter.

Ten more steps.

Gregory looked up and saw what was happening. He saw the look in Sinclair's eyes and saw where he was running.

"Don't do it! These people deserve this. They deserve it. I can help you bring Claire back!"

Five more steps.

Sinclair shielded himself from Gregory's words. Even if they were true, it didn't matter. Sinclair had to let go. He had to let go. He had to let go.

One last step.

Sinclair swung the 2x4 with all his might right at . . . Claire.

She had materialized right where Beatrice had been, her body overlapping the vision of Beatrice like a sheet over a mattress. Sinclair almost stopped his swing. He almost froze mid-attack, arced the 2x4 up over his wife's head, threw the weapon away, or something, anything else to cancel the attack.

Almost.

But he saw his wife's lips; really forced himself to look at her for the first time since her ghost had appeared. He saw the words she was mouthing. Saw that one phrase he'd been so desperate to say since the day he'd lost her. The simple moment of closure he'd been agonizing without. She was saying it now.

"Goodbye."

It let him follow through with his swing.

The board cracked against the already fractured skull of Beatrice Rochester, and this time Sinclair finished what Matty Davis had begun. The skull caved in, the entire right temple buckling like an egg smacked too hard against the corner of a countertop.

Gregory's scream was horrendous. It was guttural and it was raw and it was pure emotion unleashed into the night sky. Sinclair remembered when he'd screamed the same way in the morgue, identifying Claire's body. He knew that kind of hurt. And he was sorry.

Gregory tried to keep his grip on his wife's body, but the old, dead, fragile skin which had held his wife's skeleton together ripped under the blunt force of Sinclair's attack.

Beatrice's head fell off the roof first, quickly followed by her right arm, then some of the dislodged bones from her neck.

There was nothing Gregory could do to save her.

He swung his arms around to try to regather his crumpling wife's form but lost his balance, teetering on the edge of the roof.

There was a dark moment, as Gregory remained wobbled, where the man could have saved himself. He could have thrown his weight backwards, stayed on the roof, tried to rebuild a life without his Beatrice. But that would have been hard. That would have been painful. Never mind prison, Gregory didn't want to survive another day, another minute, another second without his beloved.

As Beatrice's puppets fell, lifeless with their conduit destroyed, Gregory made his choice.

He fell in a spiral, right shoulder caterwauling past his left hip, heels up above his head, then down below, over and over again. He still held as much of his wife's corpse in his arms as he could.

Below, the alley was full of fire. Two dumpsters had caught and had a full blaze going. The fires had already consumed Beatrice's skull by the time Gregory reached them, but the flames weren't satisfied yet. Flames never were.

There was a gross crack as Rochester's back snapped over lip of the dumpster and he folded in half; his torso and head lost in the burning trash heap where his wife's skull had fallen, his legs limp, exposed in the alley outside.

And still, somehow, he maintained his grip on Beatrice.

The pair of them burned together, as Sinclair assumed they would for the rest of eternity, long after the flames in Hollow Hills were extinguished.

# IN THE BED OF A BLUE CHEVY

**A FEW WEEKS LATER,** Sinclair sat in his house, hot coffee in his hands, watching the outside world through the safety of his blinds. Fall was in full swing by that point, with most of the leaves from the trees in his yard morphed into their seasonal browns, reds, and oranges, collected on the ground, hiding the lawn that Sinclair had finally gotten around to cutting.

Barker Davis and some other kids rode by on their bikes with smiles on their faces that showed no hint of the horrors they had endured. Were kids actually that elastic? Could they really bounce back so quickly from an event so monstrous? If so, Sinclair envied them. But he imagined the smiles were masks. Band-Aids slapped on to hide the emotional bullet holes they'd been riddled with. Wounds that some therapist would get paid lots of money to help actually heal in the not-so-distant future.

But for now baseball cards thrummed in their wheel spokes and the girl that was with them shrieked with joy as they took the hill down towards Main Street just a little too fast. A black and blue blur rushed through the trees beside them, the peacock easily keeping pace with its kid, ready to protect him at all costs. Fucking weird-ass, wonderful, dinosaur bird.

Sinclair smiled as Barker glanced at his house and shot a middle finger towards his front door.

Sinclair smiled and flicked off the kid right back before at the bike Johnny gave him, parked just inside the front door. It would start gathering dust soon, with his car fixed and operable again, and Max's car seat safely tucked away in the attic.

He sighed, cast his eyes up towards the ceiling as if he could see the car seat up there through all the planks and plaster and insulation. He would never use the damned thing again, would hopefully never even look at it again, but throwing the contraption away felt like a bridge too far. Sorting trash from keepsakes was a delicate process. One which Sinclair knew he hadn't mastered quite yet. Outside, the garbage truck rumbled around the corner right on schedule as if summoned by Sinclair's thoughts.

Sinclair sipped his coffee and diverted his attention back outside, taking one last look at the boxes from Charlotte which he'd piled on the curb. Most of the things from inside the boxes had been unpacked and arranged around the new house, set in places that felt the most like where Claire would have wanted them. Plates were on the lowest shelf in the cabinet, so she could reach them. The knife block had been pushed back into the deepest corner of the counter so Max couldn't reach them. It felt a bit silly, child-proofing a house with no children. But the exercise felt right and proper.

Sinclair was still healing.

He knew that. He was slowly making his peace with the fact that his wife and son were gone, but the process was going to be a gradual one. A matter of one more picture discarded here and one knife block perched more precariously there. Healing wasn't quick. Healing wasn't just a swift erasure of trauma from some mental, physical white board. Healing was hard work. It was painful. It was gradual. And Sinclair was learning to take it one step at a time.

Trying to go cold turkey had been stupid. He couldn't just move into a new town and pretend like Charlotte had never existed, that his family had never existed. That never would have worked, and everybody who had tried to force that approach down his throat had been wrong. In most cases, *dead* wrong.

Johnny's body had been recovered from the Sheriff's Department wreckage the morning after the incident and now his ash-covered badge sat beside Sinclair's sink. Sinclair didn't have the heart to wash it off yet, never mind putting the damn thing on.

And there was Gregory Rochester. He remembered the look in Rochester's eyes right before he fell. The desperation therein. The suffering. How he had wanted so badly for things to just be right again. Whole again with his wife. He had gone to such desperate measures to avoid healing. Sinclair couldn't go down that road. Wouldn't.

The garbage truck's brakes hissed and whined beside his mailbox. Ricky Pinecone (surely not his real name) hopped off the back of the truck, saw Sinclair through the window, and gave him a little wave before tossing the boxes into the back of the truck.

Somewhere in those boxes, Beatrice's spell book had been buried. Sinclair hadn't let himself look at it again, lest he lose his resolve. He'd just opened the drawer in the bathroom, taken the damned thing out, and thrown it in the nearest box headed to the curb.

He never had told anybody about it.

But maybe that was for the best. No more loose ends. When the trash compactor smashed those pages into piles of grey, pulpy nothingness, that would be the end of it. No sitting in an evidence locker waiting for the wrong hands to stumble across it. No copies made and distributed anywhere to be archived. No. This nightmare ended with him.

Sinclair bit back his tears and waved back as Claire's sewing kit disappeared into the green machine along with the box of some stuffed animals which Max never really played with. Sinclair still had Bear and Kitty upstairs in Max's room. Getting rid of the extra fluff had been hard enough. But one step at a time. Sinclair would get through this.

Hopefully the town would do the same.

It was a war zone downtown. Thankfully, Sinclair had overestimated the number of bodies in the streets. When all was accounted for, there were twenty-seven dead members of the town, Gregory Rochester and Johnny included. The other twenty-five all had some connection to the Gattis Lumber Mill which meant, Sinclair intended to investigate, that they all probably played some hand in Beatrice Rochester's death. Most of the town had been innocent in Beatrice's eyes, and so they had been spared by the puppets, hiding safely in their basements or merely knocked unconscious as the dolls ushered their children to the toy store, safe from the flames. What had seemed, at night, like just a broad strokes cleansing of the Hollow Hills population had actually been precise. Calculated. Targeted.

Sinclair supposed he should be thankful for that. The wicked were gone. The innocent had been spared. Damn Gregory and Beatrice to hell for playing judge, jury, and executioner, but it seemed like their actions had stayed, at least on the surface level, inappropriately justified.

All up and down the East Coast, drug cartels would be

scampering to take up the slack in the sudden power vacuum that Ethan Gattis' death had left behind. But that wasn't Sinclair's problem. Let the FBI and the DEA deal with that blowback. For Sinclair, and his new, little chunk of the world, they were getting a chance to start fresh. Hollow Hills would be deeply scarred from the events of the previous night. Physically. Emotionally. Mentally. But together, Sinclair hoped they could, over time, begin to heal again.

His coffee was empty, and Sinclair placed the mug in the sink, adjusted his belt, and slipped on his shoes. He needed to get downtown. There was lots of cleanup to oversee. He picked up his car keys from the counter without any reservations. He was just driving a car. No need to be haunted by the ghosts of his past anymore. It was just his car. He could drive it again.

And with that, Sinclair left the house. The house that was now full of his things. The house that was finally beginning to feel like a home, in a town that was finally starting to feel like a fresh start. Sinclair was finally ready to face the world again. Even if there was nothing he could do to help Claire or Max now, he could still help this town. He understood their unique brand of hurt. And he could help them rise back from it, stronger, better. Like a fucking peacock phoenix.

He chuckled a bit, feeling an inch of his former good-natured self return, and he went to work.

# THE END?

## Not if you want to dive into more of Crystal Lake Publishing's Tales from the Darkest Depths!

Check out our amazing website and online store
or download our latest catalog here.
https://geni.us/CLPCatalog

Looking for award-winning Dark Fiction?

Download our latest catalog.

Includes our anthologies, novels, novellas, collections, poetry, non-fiction, and specialty projects.

TALES FROM THE DARKEST DEPTHS

We always have great new projects and content on the website to dive into, as well as a newsletter, behind the scenes options, social media platforms, our own dark fiction shared-world series and our very own webstore. Our webstore even has categories specifically for KU books, non-fiction, anthologies, and of course more novels and novellas.

# ABOUT THE AUTHOR

William Sterling is an independent author and host of the Killer Mediums podcast. My books tend to play in the realms of "popcorn flick horror" with high body counts and a soft spot for unexpected endings.

Like Closed Room Mysteries with a touch of the Paranormal? Try *Through Frozen Veins.*

Like Small Town Horror that blows up in the third act? Try *Through Withered Roots*

Do the words "Reverse Camp Slasher" make you want to climb out of a lake with a machete? *Killer Be Killed* might be your style.

Do you crave Dystopian Sci-Fi where *Les Mis* butts heads with tech horror? *SYNAPSE* will offer you top dollar for your memories.

Want to know more? Or just keep up with my comings and goings? Follow me here on Amazon, or on Twitter @Spooky_Sterling

To contact, please email TheWilliamSterling@gmail.com

Readers . . .

Thank you for reading *String Them Up*. We hope you enjoyed this novel.

If you have a moment, please review *String Them Up* at the store where you bought it.

Help other readers by telling them why you enjoyed this book. No need to write an in-depth discussion. Even a single sentence will be greatly appreciated. Reviews go a long way to helping a book sell, and is great for an author's career. It'll also help us to continue publishing quality books. You can also share a photo of yourself holding this book with the hashtag #IGotMyCLPBook!

Thank you again for taking the time to journey with Crystal Lake Publishing.

Visit our Linktree page for a list of our social media platforms.
https://linktr.ee/CrystalLakePublishing

## Our Mission Statement:

Since its founding in August 2012, Crystal Lake Publishing has quickly become one of the world's leading publishers of Dark Fiction and Horror books in print, eBook, and audio formats.

While we strive to present only the highest quality fiction and entertainment, we also endeavour to support authors along their writing journey. We offer our time and experience in non-fiction projects, as well as author mentoring and services, at competitive prices.

With several Bram Stoker Award wins and many other wins and nominations (including the HWA's Specialty Press Award), Crystal Lake Publishing puts integrity, honor, and respect at the forefront of our publishing operations.

We strive for each book and outreach program we spearhead to not only entertain and touch or comment on issues that affect our readers, but also to strengthen and support the Dark Fiction field and its authors.

Not only do we find and publish authors we believe are destined for greatness, but we strive to work with men and woman who endeavour to be decent human beings who care more for others than themselves, while still being hard working, driven, and passionate artists and storytellers.

Crystal Lake Publishing is and will always be a beacon of what passion and dedication, combined with overwhelming teamwork and respect, can accomplish. We endeavour to know each and every one of our readers, while building personal relationships with our authors, reviewers, bloggers, podcasters, bookstores, and libraries.

We will be as trustworthy, forthright, and transparent as any business can be, while also keeping most of the headaches away from our authors, since it's our job to solve the problems so they can stay in a creative mind. Which of course also means paying our authors.

We do not just publish books, we present to you worlds within your world, doors within your mind, from talented authors who sacrifice so much for a moment of your time.

There are some amazing small presses out there, and through collaboration and open forums we will continue to support other presses in the goal of helping authors and showing the world what quality small presses are capable of accomplishing. No one wins when a small press goes down, so we will always be there to support hardworking, legitimate presses and their authors. We don't see Crystal Lake as the best press out there, but we will always strive to be the best, strive to be the most interactive and grateful, and even blessed press around. No matter what happens over time, we will also take our mission very seriously while appreciating where we are and enjoying the journey.

What do we offer our authors that they can't do for themselves through self-publishing?

We are big supporters of self-publishing (especially hybrid publishing), if done with care, patience, and planning. However, not every author has the time or inclination to do market research, advertise, and set up book launch strategies. Although a lot of authors are successful in doing it all, strong small presses will always be there for the authors who just want to do what they do best: write.

What we offer is experience, industry knowledge, contacts and trust built up over years. And due to our strong brand and trusting fanbase, every Crystal Lake Publishing book comes with weight of respect. In time our fans begin to trust our judgment and will try a new author purely based on our support of said author.

With each launch we strive to fine-tune our approach, learn from our mistakes, and increase our reach. We continue to assure our authors that we're here for them and that we'll carry the weight of the launch and dealing with third parties while they focus on their strengths—be it writing, interviews, blogs, signings, etc.

We also offer several mentoring packages to authors that include knowledge and skills they can use in both traditional and self-publishing endeavours.

We look forward to launching many new careers.

This is what we believe in. What we stand for. This will be our legacy.

**Welcome to Crystal Lake Publishing—**
**Tales from the Darkest Depths.**

Made in the USA
Coppell, TX
01 November 2023